The

Great

Gambit

Copyright © 2021 Richard Plender

The moral right of the author has been asserted.

All rights reserved.

No part of this publication may be reproduced, stored in a retrieval system, or transmitted, in any form or by any means, without the prior permission in writing of the publisher, nor be otherwise circulated in any form of binding or cover other than that in which it is published and without a similar condition including this condition being imposed on the subsequent purchaser.

ISBN: 9798489007801

The Great Gambit

RICHARD PLENDER

To Dad and Tom

Editor's note:

Due to now antiquated concepts and bizarre, verbose flourishes by the writer of this historical document, I have added various footnotes to aid the comprehension of the reader. Unfortunately, only a few remaining parts of the 'Miller Tract' remain, this extract being one of them. While the author of this record can seem arrogant and at times frustratingly didactic, we must make sure we preserve it and pass it on as secretly and safely as we can. This document contains, as far as we know, the only surviving record of Max Miller's post-sentencing testimony. It is thanks to the anonymous introduction to this testimony that we are given valuable context to the extraordinary things Max Miller describes. The following material may also be one of the last and most important clues we have left to the nature of pre-contact existence and the events that followed the landings.

- - -

There were many reasons postulated as to why, after the final touches were added to the Drake equation, alien communities had still not made contact with human civilisation. According to the equation at that time - June 9th 2051 to be precise - there were, with a confidence interval of 95%, 27,635 alien civilisations. As we now know, this estimate was astonishingly close to the real number. And, just as relativity corrected Newtonian predictions by a few decimal points, so did the Drake equation then predict the correct number of alien civilisations only a few single digits away from the truth.

As is always the case with humanity and the cavernous gills of vanity by which it breathes, we assumed aliens had deliberately not made contact because of *us*, as a species. Just like a fly who repeatedly bangs her head against the window concludes she can't get through because there's something wrong with her eyesight. We thought anthropocentrically, as we always did, and always will.

We were too pugnacious. Prone to self-destruction. Deleterious to our planet and environment. No! We were being watched, examined, allowed to progress naturally, like a sprawling fungus. No! We weren't just being watched. We were being incubated, until we were to reach that state of technological progress by which we might actually be useful to a vastly superior intergalactic community, in constant need of fuel and resources…

Of course we now know all these conjectural splutters were wrong. They just hadn't noticed we existed.

I heard of an elephant once who kept receiving letters and petitions from an unknown species with all sorts of wild demands. The letters came first, asking if the elephant could speak, whether he knew what a hive mind was, and whether he also possessed a hive mind, just like they did. The letters became increasingly desperate and finally the petitions came. Hundreds of thousands of signatures were sent to the elephant demanding that he stop ignoring them. Oh, and by the way, if he could stop treading on them every so often. Utterly baffled, the elephant never worked out what this species was, and continued to ignore them, and tread on them, until the end of his days.

The circumstances which precipitated first contact, were as it turns out, a complete accident - a freak incident that even the outliers of sub-atomic wave functions should never have allowed to happen.

It all started when Max Miller, a senior SEO strategist, embarked upon a carefully planned existential crisis. The 20th century phenomenon of the 'mid-life' crisis had somewhat ebbed during the 20s, replaced by its chic and smarter rival, the 'quarter-life' crisis. In its embryonic form this was an academic observation, a psychoanalytic buzz word. But just as with its shibboleth of a cousin, it quickly turned into a trend, followed by the inevitable corollary of all post-industrial civilisation: marketing.

The great advantage of quarter-life stricken individuals, was that they were younger and had a much higher marginal propensity to consume. Individuals in their 40s were more entrenched in their spending patterns, but quarter-lifers were more vulnerable and more prone to spend vast sums of It-Coin[1] on virtual and non-virtual goods. Social media caught on fast and before long if you weren't having, about to have, or hadn't had a quarter-life crisis you were stripped of your social citizenship. These accursed expatriates of human society were cast into a sulphurous netherworld of real things and non-virtual existence.

Max Miller, amazingly enough, had avoided this antediluvian state. He had missed the boat, being 29 when it had all taken off. A strategist by profession, he managed to manipulate his online avatar enough so that he could just about pass as a post-quarter-lifer. This was quite a feat to accomplish, given that his internet data was immutable and beyond his control.

---

1. Presumably, short for 'internet coin'.

When he brushed over his mid-twenties - filled as they were with indescribable heights of virtual ecstasy and profound life satisfaction - there were a large number of individuals who questioned his curious narrative; the idea, that all those ecstatic delights on his profile history were really just an expression of deep inner-suffering, failed to convince the more astute members of the online community. Those who had bothered to experience his voems[2], bellowing his joy and astonishment at the wonders of all things virtual and non-virtual, saw through this ad hoc revisionism. There was no quarter-life crisis to be found between the blinding binary code of ineffaceable internet data.

Max Miller, from what little we know of him, felt painfully aware that he was constantly eclipsed by the shadow of this spurious narrative. While not jettisoned to the lowest regions of social exile, he was most certainly on the lower end of the social scale. It was time for a change. An all-or-nothing gamble that could destroy or elevate him forever.

As anyone who works in marketing knows, trends peak and trough, and by thirty-eight years of age Max Miller realised that the outlook for the continued popularity of the quarter-life crisis was looking increasingly bearish. An ever burgeoning section of the population was hankering for something new - or as Max Miller shrewdly realised - something old. The mid-life crisis was going to make a comeback. He knew this was his chance. And just as with all great investors, he had been blessed both with serendipity and artful cunning. He was the perfect age, and he had the skill set to pull it off. And so he started planning, carefully and meticulously, for the grand execution

---

2. Multi-sensory virtual poems. Now obsolete.

of the perfect, real-time, mid-life crisis. Not only did he see the trend coming, he would help set it too.

So how does one execute a non-organic mid-life crisis? From a scientific angle, the most obvious way would be to set and meet the appropriate initial conditions to effect such a phenomenon. And what are those boundary conditions, those subjective tremors, that send the grinding tectonics of a person's soul into a desperate rupture of angst?

Greater thinkers than Max Miller had pondered this question. But there were certain irrefutable factors that seemed to chime unanimously through the graveyard of dead middle-aged men. There's the mind-numbing job, the soured marriage, the childhood dreams that were never tickled or sated… The problem was, Max Miller already met these conditions, and was still contented enough not to be in the depths of worry and despair: he spent his days chewing the cud of search engine optimisation; he was divorced, twice, from two husbands; he had never ridden a horse before they had become critically endangered.[3] Still, he was happy enough to continue along the same path he had always trodden, but not happy enough to stay where he was at the soggy end of the watermill.

Max Miller realised that initial conditions weren't enough. He needed to approach the problem from another angle. Firstly, his mid-life crisis would have to evolve like a tapestry online, cascading tragically from one scene to the next. Otherwise, what was the point? As with anything on the internet, to keep its attention it would have to escalate. Secondly, the issue was

---

3. Hoofed quadrupeds, once domesticated by *Homo sapiens*. Now extinct.

time sensitive; the frequency of mid-life crisis search queries was increasing rapidly. On the one hand this was a good thing, it meant his predictions had been bang on the money. On the other hand this gave him an unsettling sense of urgency, a sensation he wasn't used to in his so far cushy life.

They say that when Cicero popularised the tricolon, a device which punctuated his speeches with repetitions of three, astonished citizens and fellow quaestors asked how he had invented such a powerful and effective rhetorical trick. Allegedly, he responded: 'for 17 reasons: most people can only hold three things in their mind at one time, most people are easily influenced by the power of threes, and most people are idiots.' The quaestors went home enraptured with this new wisdom, only to realise next morning their profound and ignominious mistake.[4] Cicero's insight about the general attention span of the human race couldn't have been more prescient in this age of selfies, clicks and thumbnails. Max Miller's mid-life crisis would have to come in three acts.

Like all things subject to the voracious ether of social media, anything he did would have to spread. Like a grand and operatic mitosis his story would have to unfold and multiply across a vast conduit of contacts and bots. And how, from cute cats to celebrity meltdowns, do all such mitoses begin? Naturally, with those closest to you. That is, friends and subscribers to your virtual avatar.

Max Miller had, for most of his adult life, adhered strictly to the Principle of Correctness Variation Optimisation. This was

---

4. As far as we know this story is not in fact, in any meaningful way, true.

a marketing term used to identify individuals who managed to maintain a fixed set of friends with perfectly varying 'correctness' characteristics - that is, an online avatar with a set of friends that had a perfectly differentiated set of gender, sexuality, race, intelligence, nationality, class, religion, disability, weight, height, mental health, hair loss, income, education, accent, elocution and age characteristics. A person such as this had a significantly reduced chance of being cancelled and a doorway to a potentially vast proportion of the human population. This principle by its nature would not work were everyone to follow it, given the unequal distribution of traits like sexuality and race across the world. But Max Miller was in that elite few, that special few, who were lucky enough to be party to these magical and mysterious industry secrets.

Given that Max Miller had adhered to this principle so strictly (with the help of data analytics), this of course meant that he had no 'real' friends in any meaningful sense of the word. His online friends had been chosen by an algorithm of his making and groomed by him in order that they fitted exactly to a fully optimal collection of individuals only a perfectly politically flawless individual could have. If he had chosen friends according to his own whims, he would have been open to the accusation of bias and favouritism. This wouldn't have mattered much were he to remain insignificant amongst the many billions of other online human beings. But Max Miller wasn't about mediocrity - he wanted to go viral. In a world where being 'incorrect' carried heavy social and life-changing consequences, he could not be exposed on any level.

It is here that we should probably mention the political elephant in the room:

Cancellation.

On pre-contact planet earth, cancellation was the most forbidding and dangerous form of punishment any human being and his online personality could undergo.[5] If you were 'cancelled', your virtual online avatar was erased and you were exiled to the non-virtual world. From here you would be sent to the Greasing Fields. There you would spend the rest of your days labouring amongst all the other cancelled individuals, greasing with oil billions of labouring, rusting machines, sweating and starving under the scorching sun. Once known as the 'real' world, this bleak wasteland was unthinkable to any ordinary human being. It was here that men, women, children and all the other genders were governed like slaves by machines: machines given direct orders from the online community. Many chose to kill themselves both physically and virtually, rather than risk such an existence.[6]

The most pressing issue to resolve concerned content. In what exact form should his mid-life crisis manifest itself? Given that this vastly overrated social construct had been in vogue only a few decades before, he had a voluminous bibliography from which to choose; quitting one's job, becoming obsessed with the taxonomy of mushrooms, moving to Timbuktu, becoming a survivalist, editing Wikipedia articles, becoming staunchly religious, adopting a mental illness, joining an extremist left

---

5. The evolution of the phenomenon of cancellation is hard to trace. It seems to have first appeared during the early 21st century at universities, when keynote speakers were banned at the last minute from speaking at public events.

6. From the few extant records currently available, demographic studies on the Greasing Fields suggest that most of these slaves were actors, writers, journalists and politicians (cf. Choi & Kendelbridge 2087).

or right-wing militant group, starting a vlog…the list was endless. But helpful though these were to stoke the coals of the imagination, they were nothing but time-worn cliches, unlikely to fire the intestines of a churning online digestive system. They would all be absorbed and shat out, undigested, unliked and unshared.

For his first act, Max Miller needed something daring and outrageous; he needed to do something so reckless that only a person in the true throes of genuine madness could conceive of or do such a thing. After all, this was to be the grand opening of an even grander gamble. So he decided to begin his online charade with one of the most preposterous and unimaginable things possible: to criticise the internet.

It is worth mentioning here that at this stage in humanity's development the two statements 'to be alive' and 'to be online' were practically synonymous. The bit rate of your internet connection may as well have been the actual pulse of your physical body - with bytes for blood, a modem for a heart, and fibre optic cables for veins. Ninety-five percent of lived human experience was virtual. The remaining five percent - unplugged reality - was reserved for maintaining feeding tubes, replacing colostomy bags and catheters, checking vital signs, occasionally copulating and doing exercises to prevent muscle wastage.[7]

---

7. This is a blatant exaggeration. I believe the author here is trying to make a point rather than a scientific claim. Given the extensive body of research in this area, in aggregate, it seems fair to suggest that by 2046 virtual existence was actually closer to some 78% of all lived human experience, declining still further pre-contact. We also believe that human beings were lying about quite how much time they were spending virtually. The reality was people were offline, or 'unplugged', much more than the online community as a whole acknowledged or realised. This may help explain why 'Miller's

Certainly, there were a few eccentrics. Those who hadn't been cancelled but had chosen to live a life deprived of virtual sustenance - exactly the sort of thing someone experiencing a mid-life crisis would do. These individuals were generally left to themselves and had unusually low life-expectancies.

Then of course, there was cancellation - a constant reminder of why it was always propitious to stay on the better side of the internet.

So when Max Miller released his first profile update in two years, he did so knowing he would be dancing a deadly tango with the social daggers of a dangerous and capricious partner. To fall or stumble at any stage was death. He would have to judge, measure and anticipate every step, every inclination, every change of mood, with the precision of the Hubble Space Telescope. The art of judging public reaction is a pastime best left to geniuses or blessed idiots. Of which category Max Miller was is up for debate.

This profile update proved to be such a famous and momentous event, it became an accepted figure of speech in common parlance - 'a Miller moment'.

This profile update was:

'Fuck the Internet. Cancel me.'

His friends and subscribers were dumbstruck just as Max Miller had hoped. It was this 'correct' realm of acquaintances that was

---

Great Gambit', as it is now known, took off so readily when it did.

to form the Archimedean point from which the ballooning of his ambitious designs would come to fruition. Who knows what Max Miller could have been feeling, before he pressed send on that fateful second, at that particular minute, knowing that in one fell swoop his whole life could be cancelled, and he could be sent to the Greasing Fields. To look back and ponder such a moment, it is hard not to conclude that Max Miller had transcended the superficial gestures of facade and migrated to the genuine motions of real and true crisis. That, or he really was a genius.

So how could the sum of five words demand the attention of the sum of the whole online community? The answer is that to say anything less offensive, but nevertheless sacrilegious, would have meant near instant cancellation. But this statement was so bold - so audacious - that the online community had been knocked sideways, by an eight-syllable hammer, into a stupor. The public imagination, for the first time, had been unanimously bludgeoned into a state of live self-reflection. An extract from one archived thread reads:

'Who is Max Miller? #change'

'break the chains! #cancelme'

'If you cancel him, cancel me too! #cancelme'

'sometimes public opinion isn't freeing, it's IMPRISONING #cancelme'

'You can't cancel all of us. #iammaxmiller'

'do any of u guys remember when we used to drink that thing…what was it called, juice! from that glass thingy? #imissrealfood #iammaxmiller'

'Whatever happened to Greta Thunberg? REALLY? #conspiracy #iammaxmiller'

'I'm sick of feeding tubes! #cancelme'

'i think it's gr8 we're all equal But cancellation has gone TOO far. #cancelme'

'i miss taking a shit. #cancelme'

Within minutes, Max Miller's update had been viewed by half the globe. Up until this point the internet had managed to regulate itself perfectly to the imperious tune of Marketing and its spoilt cousin, Correctness. Something was shifting in the virtual public psyche. Just as minutes turned into hours that turned into days, hundreds turned into thousands that turned into millions. Max Miller's profile update had touched a nerve, and suddenly the rigidity of this system of correctness and cancellation stood naked before us in all its cruelty. The internet had started rebelling against itself. The three most shared hashtags 48 hours after the update were '#cancelme', '#unplugme' and '#iammaxmiller'.

The obvious question to ask is why they didn't unplug themselves. My own theory is that human beings were bound to the organism of cyberspace like the reticulated veins of a leaf. To extract themselves was impossible. For the first time, they had begun to understand the prison they had constructed for themselves only to realise that they hadn't built a lock or a set of keys with which to open it. Why bother with keys, locks and jailers when you have built the prison around you for yourself?

It goes without saying, there was a second important reason. There's nothing human beings like more than to revel in the delicious excesses of chaos. And what is chaos but entertainment? Everyone wanted to watch this viral awakening unfold and arrive at its inscrutable destination, wherever that may be. It is in our cultural programming to seek complication followed by denouement.

Even Max Miller, the mastermind himself, was surprised at the speed with which his update percolated through cyberspace. He was receiving friend requests by the millions and just as countless invitations to speak at virtual seminars and give press interviews. But Max Miller, the shrewd marketeer that he was, knew that to accept or give in to any of these demands, no matter how much they might polish his ego, would be a brash error of judgement. The avalanche of public sensation would be carried by its own snowballing momentum. There was nothing he could add to this natural process without slowing it down or causing problems for himself.

For his second act, Max Miller realised that if he wanted to remain topical, the best thing to do was what was instinctively quite difficult in such a situation, when you are receiving such a gratifying amount of attention: to simply disappear. This would immerse his persona in mystery, and for a certain period of time - if judged absolutely perfectly - could consecrate him with almost mythological status. There is nothing the public likes more than an enigma on which to speculate. And when speculation turns into conspiracy, you know you've hit the jackpot. You will be ordained among the rest of the online pantheon of immortal sensations, like Elvis Presley and John F Kennedy. To have your statue placed amongst these hallowed individuals was a true feat indeed. Remaining topical on the internet is futile without a priest and his augurs of conspiracy to bless you.

Needless to say, of all the three acts of Max Miller's Great Gambit, this was the most logistically and technically difficult to achieve. Not only would he have to erase himself virtually, he would have to remove himself physically too. If he wasn't tracked down in cyberspace, he could be tracked down in person. To this day no one knows where Max Miller disappeared to. His instincts however had been right, and it wasn't long before journalists, fans and curious members of the public began knocking on his door, both virtually and physically. To their dismay, by this point he was long gone.

Various profiles of Max Miller's character were drawn up by the online community. Most of his data, right up until that fateful profile update, was in the public domain. Anything that wasn't was quickly hacked and disseminated. Not much was gleaned from these pieces of information. He seemed like a perfectly normal, astonishingly correct individual. His 'friends' were interviewed, only to be found to have not known Max Miller in any meaningful way at all (as I have explained, unbeknownst to the public, they had been chosen by an algorithm). His employers at GenerationMarketing seemed to know very little about him either, but that he had brought large productivity gains to their search engine optimisation department.

Sure enough, conspiracy followed. Max Miller had been abducted and killed by the influencers - they had most to lose after all. No! He had committed suicide, terrified at the prospect of being cancelled. No! He was never a person in the first place, he had been artificially created by a secret organisation called Fiber Cutters.[8] They had used this weapon to destabilise and destroy the internet.

Like all conspiracy theories, there was a drop of truth in all of them. Indeed, the influencers - who conducted and shaped the psychological movements of nearly the whole virtual community - were profoundly unnerved. The likelihood is Max Miller probably would have been killed if he hadn't staged his spectacular disappearance as quickly as he did.

There is some disagreement about what Max Miller really did during the ten months he went silent. While most believe this was a carefully managed and calculated part of his plan, there are still those who maintain he really was going through some sort of critical emotional upheaval. It is possible that Max Miller really did panic and that he was going through exactly the sort of crisis he had so carefully engineered. Given the unbounded horizon of cyberspace and its sweeping vision of surveillance, it is still hard to believe he wasn't detected. One possibility is that he went to South America, which was largely uninhabited and contained 87% of the Earth's trees. Indeed, some eccentrics believe he spent time there with the indigenous tribes of the Amazon, some of the few non-virtual individuals left, drawing inspiration for his third and final act. However, there are no flight records or any other locational fragments of evidence

---

8. Fiber Cutters (FC) did actually exist as a distinct organised, 'terrorist' entity. It wasn't a fictional group, as many thought at the time.

that give support to this supposition. Either Max Miller found innovative ways of expunging the details of his movements or he had help.

What we do know is that wherever he was, he was working on the project that was to form the final part of his Great Gambit. Max Miller later claimed that the inspiration for the project had hit him like a flash of lightning on his 40th birthday, a month after he had disappeared. He described the experience as akin to being slapped by a birthday present addressed from God. Looking back now, it is hard not to conclude that were it not for this lethal inspiration, the fate of the human race could have looked starkly different.

Over the next nine months as Max Miller put this idea to pen and paper, the internet stewed in a vat of simmering anticipation. Some sort of revolution had started but to where it was leading no one had the faintest idea. Nearly everyone was calling for their own cancellation but no one was in fact being cancelled or unplugging themselves.

The reason that no one was being cancelled was intimately intertwined with the mechanics of cancellation itself. The process of cancellation was essentially a democratic phenomenon. Cancellation protocol was started when enough online users reported a profile for 'incorrect' behaviour and content. Incorrect behaviour covered a wide variety of immoral behaviours: maybe you had mistakenly used the wrong pronoun just one too many times; or maybe you had said you were 'starving' when in fact your BMI was well above 18.5; or just maybe, you had been a tad ageist. When a certain number had been reached an algorithm would go through a rigorous process of analysis, checking each user who had reported the unhappy individual, filtering out bots and trolls as it did so. If, after this procedure, there was still a sufficient number of 'incorrect content reports' the accused's avatar was cancelled and he was 'collected' by the appropriate authorities.[9] He could be sure to be greeting the blistering heat of the Greasing Fields the very following morning.

The online community had been brought to a state of paralysis. So long as users were calling for - and at the same time fearing - their own cancellation, they were reluctant to cancel anyone else, who was going through exactly the same thing. Previously, criticising the internet had been incorrect, but now that everyone was doing it, it had become precisely the opposite.

Naturally, there was a backlash. The influencers weren't going to back down without a fight. Valerie Craft (as she was known online), an influencer who had made her name 'outing' other influencers for incorrect behaviour, saw worrying signs in this wave of revolutionary feeling. To her detractors she was known as 'the crooked bitch' - the sexist epithet referring to an abnormality in her neck, which forced her resting head position to be slanted awkwardly to the left. Valerie Craft began a vicious campaign against Max Miller. That is, not against Max Miller the real person - who no one really knew - but the straw man the internet had created of him.

In the decades leading up to contact, power - who had it, where it was, how it was distributed - was a nebulous and amorphous

---

9. The use of the word 'authorities' here is both a euphemism and an anachronism. 'Collection' was carried out by 'extractors', machines who received commands from the CA (Central Algorithm). Apart from arguably the CA itself there were no 'authorities' to speak of.

force. Since the dismantling of the internet, we can only really make educated guesses and acknowledge that of all the different schools of thought, the reality is probably a complicated mix of all of them.[10]

Valerie Craft had made her name exploiting that hidden line between what was correct and what was not. Her followers were like soldier ants, frenzied in their instincts to implement her despotic will. This queen of political righteousness had only to point her sceptre and her colony of zealots got to work - the victim would be cancelled forthwith. The majority of these victims were fellow influencers - fashion icons, pop stars and entertainers. To people like Valerie Craft the currency of power was exhaustive. Clout was a finite resource regulated by the invisible hand of human frivolity and the gravity of marketing. So long as someone else had influence, she had less of it. In this sense she was the ultimate mercantilist, a consummate hoarder of prestige and privilege.

---

10. Without a doubt, the Central Algorithm was responsible for implementing the unwritten constitution of the internet. In the early years its code was open source and updated on a second-by-second basis by active users. However, there was a huge caveat to this seemingly democratic process. There was a whole section of the CA's code that was locked and inaccessible to the online community. It was this very section which regulated the physical world and the machines that administered to it. Here there is some confusion. It is possible the Central Algorithm locked this part of its code itself, realising that it could monitor and maintain the homeostasis of the earth better than human beings. Human beings would decide what the conditions were for being 'cancelled' in virtual society but they would never be able to alter the punishment. Coding for the Greasing Fields, and all that took place in physical reality could not be altered by normal members of the public; not long after the AI-2037 singularity, it edited and improved its own code entirely by itself. (For a more extensive discussion on the aetiology and evolution of the CA see Veyevsky and Strolek 2081.)

There is an anecdote about Valerie Craft which has become something of a myth.

She was born in 2025 in former Texas over five years before the virtual revolution had taken off. Her parents were farmers and god-fearing traditionalists. Her father in particular was dismayed at the cultural landscape and hoped that he could raise his daughter to be immune from the liberal inclinations he believed were infesting the modern world. He steeped his daughter in the Bible and tried his best to instil in her a deep fear of all that was ungodly. Principally: homosexuality, blacks and promiscuity. As with all parents of that generation they had little knowledge of, or control over, what their children could do and understand with the internet. By the age of ten she had hacked her parents' social media accounts and discovered they were both members of the Klu Klux Clan.[11] Steeped in the Bible though she was, her real convictions had already been moulded by the mores and attitudes of social media. She had both her parents arrested by the police. Her ruthless genius was to realise so early on that true authority lay with binary, and not biblical, scripture. Only six years later she had become the Mahatma Gandhi of political faultlessness. She had managed to get both her parents cancelled and sent to the newly established Greasing Fields.

So when Max Miller, this apparently utterly correct individual, began implementing his mid-life crisis, Valerie Craft was faced with a huge challenge. Her hands were tied. His online history and his choice of friends was beyond reproach. All shades of minority traits were perfectly balanced over his impeccable list

---

11. The Klu Klux Clan was a white supremacist organisation founded in the 1860s. Towards the end of the 2020s the organisation had entirely dissolved.

of acquaintances. She saw that this abrupt change of character had been expertly managed. There was no dirt her soldier ants could dig up with which she could smear him.

At first, Valerie Craft came to the conclusion that she would not be able to track Max Miller down personally by any clandestine means. Instead she waged an online war against Max Miller, calling him out for 'disruption of the online constitution'. Many influencers quickly fell into line - more out of fear than anything else. She used the collective might of her online following to cancel as many sympathisers with the Max Miller cause as she could.

Unfortunately for Valerie Craft, by this point, Max Miller was ready to complete the final stage of his gambit: the release of his magnum opus. This was the cornerstone from which an unfortunate confluence of disconnected events splattered its grim paint over the portrait of humanity's future. It is now considered, along with the discovery of nuclear fission, possibly the most catastrophic invention made and conceived of by humankind.

This 'invention' was in fact not really an invention at all. Max Miller, by chance or intention, was attuned to the reactionary public mood. He had brought back the mid-life crisis, and now he felt ready to bring back something even more ancient and fundamental: the novel.

The novel had died a slow but silent death some decades previously after The Big Proliferation[12]. Apart from a few

---

12. The exponential expansion of social media from the 2000s to the 2030s.

peculiar groups and individuals, nearly the whole of fiction as a medium of expression had been wiped out.

Creation is a curious phenomenon. Before the internet, objects given life by the ambitious strides of human imagination were adapted and sculpted for the pleasure of humankind. The internet however, like Frankenstein's monster, drew breath upon its completion. It was alive and able to interact with the human race as a distinct living entity. In this way, it wasn't the internet that adapted for the pleasure and entertainment of human beings, but human beings who adapted themselves to the internet. Our attention spans became shorter and all forms of time-consuming art died. The only pitiful fragments of literature that continued to thrive after this extinction were vacuous and badly constructed adolescent instapoetry.[13]

This Golem we called the internet, fashioned from the mud of greed and myopic ambition, fastened our brains to a conveyer belt of creative atrophy. We swam through it like goldfish in a bowl, in a constant state of semi-distraction. Our brains processed entertainment in discrete 3-second packets, like a surface receives the indivisible quanta of light. It was as if we were children again, reduced to a stupor of simplicity in response to a world so terrifyingly complex. How could a structure like the novel remain stable under such harsh conditions? It turns out Max Miller had the answer.

After ten months of hibernation, Max Miller returned to cyberspace. His message to the online community is well

---

[13]. For a sweeping review of early-mid 21st century instapoetry and the death of literary standards see Crawley and Fitch 2109.

documented, but for the sake of posterity I have taken the trouble to copy it here.

**Man is born free and everywhere he is in chains.
www.maxmiller.com #maxmiller #fucktheinternet**

Attached to this invocation of one of those grand old thinkers was the hyperlink - the pandora's box - that would soon precipitate that critical and fateful visit: first contact. This seemingly innocuous link directed all users who clicked on it - and that was pretty much everybody - to the fruits of his ten month hiatus: the first novel written in three decades. The reaction was unprecedented. If Max Miller's first pivotal tweet ten months previously had been something of an earthquake, this was a gravity-defying, unrestricted tsunami. His novel took off, largely thanks to the ravenous attention garnered by the enigma he had become.

Cultural paradigm shifts usually depend upon a change in the zeitgeist. That is, a dramatic shift in phase in the wave of public consciousness, expressed across a spectrum of thinkers and everyday citizens. What was so extraordinary about Max Miller's Great Gambit was that the cultural paradigm had shifted as a result of just him, one man. Like a deus ex machina, Max Miller's novel flashed into violent existence and hacked the threads of our collective narrative plot. The human race would never be the same again.

The novel was called The Plight of the Minnivih.[14]

---

14. Post-contact, The Plight of the Minnivih was purposefully and wantonly completely eradicated. Never before has a work of literature gone through such an extensive and calculated annihilation. Those of us who are still

Unfortunately, Max Miller's novel is now lost. But we have enough clues from secondary sources to acquire some sort of rudimentary understanding of what Max Miller's momentous novel was about. Grand stories have forever served both a complimentary and destructive function, both supporting and subverting arrogant systems that put claims on the meaning of our lives and the functioning of society. They enrich and disparage the false consciousness of a given epoch. From Virgil's Aeneid to Dante's Inferno, they simultaneously reinforce and destroy systems of thought, ritual and belief. In this way, Max Miller's novel was no different. What he didn't know was that in fact he was destroying and reinforcing a system lightyears outside the parochial context of planet earth - humanity's defiled playground.

I heard of an artilleryman once who received a confusing order from his superior. In the midst of some vicious and decisive battle, his commander - a boorish, aristocratic man, with a penchant for violence - ordered him to turn his canon, the most destructively powerful weapon in the regiment, and fire it at their own military headquarters. The poor subordinate was baffled. Against military code he questioned the commander about what possible use this could do. In response, the commander laughed maniacally and pointed to the sky. Knowing better than to ask a second time, the artilleryman did what he was told and blasted their military headquarters - a sturdy fortress made of solid rock - to smithereens. The effect of this was to cause

---

working *under the veil* still hope that one day we will find if not a fragment, then a sentence from the most important book to come into existence since the Bible. Due to the highly dangerous nature of writing about The Plight of the Minnivih most of what we know about the book has been ascertained from secondary sources and oral transmission.

such considerable confusion on both sides, an armistice and an earnest period of discussion were agreed to. Unfortunately, the catastrophic effect of this blast had ruptured the planet to its core and disrupted the electromagnetic field. As a result, the sky collapsed on everyone and they all died.

Did Max Miller have any idea what his grand project was leading to? With the conceit of hindsight bias, it is tempting to look back and think Max Miller had planned this grand piece of theatre all along - right down to the most vigorous of apparently unintended consequences. But anyone who knows what happened to Max Miller, knows that this cannot be true.

The Plight of the Minnivih was probably so successful because of its allegorical nature. It struck a note with the virtual public in a way we ourselves will probably never understand. The novel described 25 years in the life of an alien witnessing the enslavement of her own race. It is a story of oppression, slavery and violence. We have a fairly detailed account of its narrative thanks to both oral and written records by post-contact survivors.

I will attempt a synopsis from what little information we have.

The Minnivih had always been a functional and peaceful people. There was nothing particularly special about them technologically or scientifically compared to other life forms they peacefully coexisted with. They enjoyed moderate space travel but not at a transgalactic level, and they really preferred to stay on their own planets and moons rather than venture out into less familiar regions of space. By other aliens they were considered self-centred and egocentric, far more obsessed with themselves than the fascinating - and frankly far more superior - civilisations they were neighbours to.

The novel centres on a figure named Mieyhah, who we will call 'she' for ease of expression and according to oral tradition. The beginning of the story centres round her relationships with two love rivals in what seems to presage a harmless and frivolous sci-fi romance. Mieyhah, by anthropoid standards, is a sweet and endearing character - not unlike a human being, with her characteristic virtues and subtle flaws. Her largest defect is her frivolousness, as she switches between one love rival to another, constantly playing them off against each other as she can't decide herself who she truly loves.

But half way through the narrative a disturbing change occurs in Mieyhah's psychology. It starts gradually and subtly, like a tiny convulsing worm, lodged irritably in some cramped cocoon at the back of her brain. She begins finding seemingly unconscious or easy decisions increasingly difficult to make, as if there is some introspective force pulling her back. That is not a force from the outside, but from within herself. As the days pass, and the love rivals become increasingly further and further away from her thoughts, the changes take on a darker and darker dimension. From finding decisions difficult - like which love rival to choose - she feels an increasing desire to go against what she would have naturally wanted to do. This strange, interminable itch in her brain and mind grows by the day, and before long - under the strange power of this force - she breaks off contact with both her lovers. She realises that what is happening is not some illness or foreign agent causing her to act out: her brain is evolving rapidly, selectively, and turning on itself.

By this point in the story, Mieyhah's mind is in a truly fractured state. Part of her brain has evolved and is telling the older parts of her brain to shut up and get with the program. At first it is over small things, like which clothes to wear, or what beverage to drink, that Mieyhah feels confused. She argues with herself, like she never would have done before, as the evolving part of her brain battles with the older ones. Her identity fragments and before long she is in crisis, as the evolving part of her encephalitic system eats and subjugates the old her. She finds herself losing interest in all the Minnivih around her and becomes increasingly obsessed with her body - her toes, her fingers, her arms, her legs, her face. The old Mieyhah doesn't want to do this of course, and we can imagine that Max Miller went into great existential detail about this internal biological crisis.

The following is an extract, written down and recorded by one of the first-generation, post-contact survivors:

Before long Mieyhah is completely enslaved to herself. She is obsessed with herself to such a point that she has forgotten even the names of her family. The evolving part of her encephalitic system has won, and there are barely any regions left of her brain - or mind - that resemble the old her. Her brain, she realises, in one rare moment of clarity, has eaten itself and now she is a slave to this new mind. The new mind is selfish, greedy and insatiable - a hundred times more so than before. She eats and eats and eats. She forgets language, society and even her own name. She stares at her body constantly and dreams of copulating with herself. But very occasionally, maybe once a moon-cycle, she feels an ancient throb, just ever so distinctly. Sometimes it is just a familiar tingling - transitory but insistent, familial but remote. Sometimes it is like an echo, dancing meekly through dark and hollow caverns. It always dies – this echo, and this tingling – swept away by some unstoppable cortical river. After more days, and more moon-cycles, the echo finally stops. Mieyhah at this stage in the story, having lost the entirety of her selfhood, rapes and eats herself in a final act of forgetful self-obsession.

Before long the rest of her race find themselves subjected to the same fate. By some strange biological singularity, evolution had compressed itself, sped itself up and run awry in the brains of these poor aliens. As their brains eat and replace their former selves, subjecting them to a 'new normal' of hunger and self-obsession, the aliens, drooling and dribbling, rape and eat themselves to near extinction.

Finally, in a rare instance of kind alietarianism, the intergalactic community intervenes and saves the last remaining Minnivih. Usually conservative and reluctant to intervene, the alien community realises things had gone too far. As egocentric and inward-looking as the Minnivih had always been, not even they deserved this extreme fate. There is such a thing as cosmic irony, but there is a fine line between farce and unacceptable tragedy. With the aid of vastly superior technology, they evacuate the last of the Minnivih and are able to stall and disrupt this destructive evolutionary process. The survivors lived on as itinerant refugees, preaching to the intergalactic community lest their sombre story be forgotten.[15]

---

15. It is impossible to verify the accuracy of the writer's retelling of Max Miller's narrative. Scholarly estimates of the length of Max Miller's novel range from 41,000 - 120,000 words. Given the entire eradication of Max Miller's novel, sadly, we will never know what it really and truly contained. From other documents we have - one of which will be revealed later in this record - we have a fairly in-depth understanding of what was probably Max Miller's prose style.

The novel was a sensation. Quite how we don't know, given the short duration of all other forms of entertainment at that point in time. There was of course a tiny elite, who had continued to read books after The Big Proliferation, but it does not seem to have been this minute few who were responsible for the astonishing popularity of the novel. We will never fully understand why Max Miller's novel was as popular as it was, given the somewhat vague and unimpressive content of its plot. One likely reason for its widespread success, asides from striking a chord in the public mood, was that Max Miller had already created an aura around himself and whatever he did. This couldn't have been achieved without the three step sequence of his gambit: rebellion, enigmatic disappearance and messianic resurgence.

Literally millions of threads ensued discussing the novel and its allegorical power. The whole existence of the internet, what it was doing to humanity, and what it was doing to the integrity of the self, was questioned. With this book, Max Miller was revered as a prophet - a seer who had pierced the false veneer of the internet and the narcissism of the human race. Indeed, looking back, it is hard not to view Miller's Great Gambit as a unity - as one elegant theatrical piece of art. Twentieth century 'postmodernists' before him had had the insight to recognise that when the boundary between reality and representation is broken down any object or performance was a potential artistic entity. The 'artistic endowment' an object had was directly proportional to the 'artist' that produced it. Max Miller had taken this postmodern idea and thrust it beyond the stuffy limits of place, time and space: his whole life itself was one magnificent work of art. He had turned his prosaic, boring life into an audacious artistic performance. Alas, as I'm sure all great painters know, sometimes paintings themselves take on lives and meanings far beyond their control.

Of course, not everyone was happy with Max Miller's veiled criticisms of the internet. Valerie Craft and her sycophantic crew of influencers saw the existential threat. Their initial response was to ignore the novel completely, but when they witnessed the book take off like a bank run, they realised that something had to be done. If readership managed to reach a certain critical mass, there would be nothing she could do. Her currency of influence would be irreparably devalued.

She had one advantage however, and that was that Max Miller was now an online personage once again. Now he was plugged back in, he was locatable. You just can't hide data. While Valerie Craft was seen as the founding symbol of the 'correctness' revolution, she was by no means averse to 'creative', if not questionable methods. Valerie Craft was aware that there was no way to cancel Max Miller, he was far too popular. What she needed was some good, old-fashioned, under-the-counter, brawn. She secretly enlisted the services of an underground paramilitary group and set about exterminating Max Miller.

Needless to say they never found Max Miller. How do we know this? We know this because on the 5th of April 2069, in what came to be known as Silent Wednesday, seven armed men were found slaughtered and dismembered at an address in Jasper, a small town situated amidst the forbidding peaks of the Canadian Rockies. Found on their bodies were handwritten personal instructions from Valerie Craft.[16] No one knew who killed

---

16. Black market contracts were probably always handwritten, given that they could easily be destroyed and did not leave a digital footprint. Most

them or even how. No one even heard it happen. According to prevailing public opinion at the time, Max Miller had nothing to do with it whatsoever. There was no evidence he had been anywhere near the scene of the crime.[17] An attempted assassination and murder on such a scale had not occurred in the public eye for some years and the internet reacted with stunned silence, followed by vengeful indignation.

Max Miller had been elevated from revered revolutionary to god-like status since the release of his novel. Max Miller's first act - to defiantly demand cancellation - was seen as a daring and ironic protestation. Ever since, the phenomenon of cancellation became increasingly the diminished domain of influencers attached to Valerie Craft. The population had recognised cancellation for what it was: a barbaric social cleansing mechanism. The human race, having fumbled and cast about in the dark, at last found its contact lenses. It looked around in dismay and saw that it had been sleeping soundly in a blood-stained sieve. The deepest irony of all, was that the last act of cancellation sanctioned by members of the online community was of Valerie Craft herself. Her cronies pooled what little resources (subscribers) they had left and cancelled

---

people under the age of 50 by 2068 couldn't write by hand, it was a skill primarily learned by criminals and historians. Valerie Craft was an exception in this regard, given her unusually conservative christian upbringing.

17. Again, the use of the word 'crime' here is a misnomer, and probably a reflection of post-contact attitudes and terminology. By 2068 law on planet earth as a stable, absolutist institution didn't exist. Machines in non-virtual reality, which implemented the 'general will' of the online community, were guided by fluid and rapidly changing public opinion mediated through the Central Algorithm, meaning that what was permissible one minute might not have been permissible the next. Certainly, these machines were enforcers - but when law has become continuous, and is no longer discrete, to what extent are we able to call that 'law'?

her, fearing that were she to remain virtually alive the public would investigate them and turn on them too. It was a necessary act of self-preservation.

The Plight of the Minnivih had changed everything. It was considered along with the creations of William Shakespeare, Wolfgang Amadeus Mozart and Leonardo Da Vinci as a supreme work of genius. Never mind that the human race at that time might have confused political ramifications for creative brilliance, they nevertheless sent it into space should it one day be intercepted or found by intelligent life from other planetary systems. They also sent, along with Max Miller's book, a record of Autobahn by Kraftwerk, and a small quantity of ancient Chinese gunpowder from the tenth century.

At this critical point in the history of *Homo sapiens*, the benefits of technological progress were questioned for the very first time. Nostalgic glances were cast back to former centuries where legislatures, courts and executives existed. The internet had become a victim of its own insatiable progress and humanity had finally become ready to leave it behind. We had to retrace our steps and find a different path, even if that meant abandoning so much convenience and so much information. The problem was there wasn't much of a world to go back to. Technological progress had damaged vast areas of the biosphere. The Central Algorithm had attempted to slow global warming, and it had planted vast numbers of trees via the work of its tens of millions of machines. But the fact was, the earth was still unbearably hot, which is why all these machines had needed so much greasing. What they did have, however, was something the human race had been bereft of for a very, very long time. That is: God.

When Nietzsche made his famous statement that 'God is Dead' in 1882 he was not speaking metaphysically. He was talking of the cultural attitudes of modern Western society and the post-enlightenment dismantling of religion with its promise of absolute morality. He foresaw disastrous consequences were we not to install 'sacred games' and 'festivals of atonement' in its place. Had social media not turned into a sacred game of strict and punishing social commandments? Had cancellation not become its own festival of atonement? Indeed they had, and the human race had paid dearly for this false substitution. Nietzsche finishes the passage by asking a question: must we ourselves not become Gods to match the loss of such an entity?

Apparently yes we must, because Max Miller certainly did.

Vast numbers of the population began unplugging themselves. This wasn't a 'hot' revolution as such since the internet, as far as we know, and the technology that supported its survival, was not actually destroyed. It was more a solemn denunciation, as if we had all woken up with a terrible hangover after a long night of revelling, had covered our eyes with our hands, looked at the floor, shaken our heads in disbelief, and walked out of the room. Humanity wanted to forget this disturbing episode and banish it forever from its collective psyche. Unfortunately, as has always been the case over the course of the entire history of our species, when we abandon the jurisdiction of higher powers and prime movers - be that ideology or religion - we are but wayward children running amok through dense and unnavigable forest. We become orphans looking for new adoptive parents. We never need to search for long. The human race seems to have an innate creative genius for displacement activity.

So it was Max Miller's turn now to become the new moral abacus. A cult of personality emerged along with new and strange customs. The Plight of the Minnivih became biblical in its reach and authority, as people across the globe read and reread it until they could remember large chunks of it off by heart. Max Miller's entire data history was shared and disseminated widely, with photos and printouts of his past communications adorning the walls of every home and dwelling. The fall of the social media machine was like the fall of an empire, with a period of renewal marked by smaller groups and collectives. There is even evidence that on the fringes some communities branched off into more fanatical autonomous groups, with contemporaneous chroniclers referring to 'exotic dances, prayer and human sacrifice'. Meanwhile, in most areas, a vast reconstruction took place and large swathes of human beings reconciled themselves with returning to a more basic form of existence. Municipal buildings were reconstructed, artefacts such as books and DVDs were collected, even various extinct physical sports were revived, such as 'football' and 'hockey'. Whether to describe this period as a time of 'renewal' or a return to 'medievalism' depends on where one looks geographically.[18]

---

18. The period of Reconstruction and return to physical reality has been studied widely by contemporary academics. It seems that in most communities technology, and even the internet, was not totally abandoned. Frustratingly, we have scant source material on the nature of political organisation during this period, leaving important questions about how unplugged society was organised unanswered. If the Central Algorithm no longer co-ordinated all social behaviour, surely human civilisation would have split into groups as the author describes, reverting back to older hierarchical forms of government such as autocracy, oligarchy and democracy. This would have undoubtedly led to civil strife and international conflict. Strangely enough, conflict seems to have been minimal, and apart from fringe groups, most of human civilisation remained surprisingly peaceful and coordinated. We have two competing, but not mutually exclusive, theories as to why this

Max Miller wholeheartedly embraced his new position, and he travelled the globe giving speeches and lectures. He gave many public readings of his novel, which served as a constant reminder as to why the internet should remain in its place. A sort of intellectual revolution took place as interest in law, history, culture, written constitutions and social heterogeneity across human civilisation resurfaced. Culture and identity as a variegated and sometimes competing set of norms, with necessary differences, characteristics and tensions, reemerged. A debate about technology ensued, with public assemblies - that is, at actual physical places - not unlike those of ancient Greece. In line with Max Miller's preaching it was agreed that technology should not be abandoned but reexamined. Even the terminology used about technology needed to change. No one doubted that technology contained advantages if it was used in an appropriate manner but that unchecked innovation for the sake of it was an outdated dogma. The phrase 'technological progress' was deemed entirely misleading and ideological. Innovation was not the same as progress if it led to adverse moral consequences. The Greasing Fields were shut down and in the years that followed the release of Max Miller's novel there was most certainly a cheerful sense of optimism.[19]

---

might have been the case. The first is that the cult of personality and quasi-religious practice surrounding Max Miller was so universal that it bound the human race socially and staved off sectarianism. The second and much less fanciful theory is that the Central Algorithm continued existing in a limited capacity, helping to co-ordinate human beings with logistics and assisting with Reconstruction.

19. One of the frustrating things about this historical extract is the lack of detail. How were the Greasing Fields 'shut down' exactly? They received commands from the Central Algorithm. Again, we find ourselves asking what happened to the Central Algorithm itself. Presumably, if the internet was not entirely destroyed as the author attests, it still existed. Like all historical documents this whole account is riddled with bias and omission.

But it was short lived.

By some miraculous confluence of minuscule probabilities - extreme and remote contingencies that should never have conspired together, let alone have happened on their own - the robotic probe known as Voyager 3 was intercepted by alien intelligent life just as it was approaching the speed of light. As we now know, only five years since Voyager 3 had departed from planet earth, it had been intercepted by an alien reconnaissance probe in our very own backyard. We had always assumed that those 27,635 civilisations predicted by the Drake equation were scattered in realms of the universe we could never possibly hope to explore. We had not accounted for the fact that no matter how far away they were, their own scientific technology could mean they were much closer to us than we had ever expected. We had seriously underestimated our peripatetic neighbours. Unfortunately for us, it was this very Voyager 3 that contained Max Miller's world changing novel. If we had not been seduced by this one act of hubris - of blasting our cultural litter into space - maybe planet earth and its incipient moral renaissance could have bloomed and flourished.

Humanity of course had no idea what had happened. What they did know was that for some unaccountable reason all communications with Voyager 3 had abruptly halted. Concerns were raised but no tears were shed. After all, the probe had

---

It reads like an allegory rather than good history. The author constantly makes generalisations and lofty assertions about the human race, as if he himself were some sort of authority on the subject - not unlike Tactitus and Livy when they wrote their own histories of Rome. That said, we know from other documents proven to have been written by different authors, that the fundamental strain of this narrative is most probably, more or less true.

always been more of a statement than a question. Eight months passed without note and Voyager 3 was practically forgotten.

On July the 4th 2076, on the 300th anniversary of American Independence Day, alien life forms made first contact with planet earth.

*

As one contemporary Russian poet described the event:

We saw before we heard,
And ran before we thought,
As the fierce fingers of God,
Stabbed the earth like lightning.

After the terrible sight,
Came the terrible sound,
As the Earth shattered,
Spluttering rough fragments around us.

But it was not God,
Who had made us,
To our hovels,
Scurry like frightened ants.

It was not by His judgement,
We would be sentenced,
Condemned,
And tried.

No.

It was They.

They had come to count the balance,
They had come to reckon with our dust.
It is not a He, but a They,
Who 'taketh up the isles' as such little things.

We ignored Aesop and his fable of the frogs to our peril. In our constant search for God, maybe we should have been happy with the plank of wood religion had given us; we could ignore or spit on it as much as we pleased. Instead, prone to dissatisfaction as we always are, we had to prod the cosmos until it sent water serpents to devour us.

We were not visited by one but 18,000 alien life forms, each one a representative of his, her, or its race. They had all landed in the Taiga, in the depths of Siberia, where they had caused a considerable amount of destruction as a result of their landing. The catastrophic aftermath of this event caused significant geological damage as far as Malaysia and former Ghana. Were we not to succumb to the fate these aliens had already decided for us, it is likely vast swathes of planet earth would have been uninhabitable anyway.

Most human beings at the time never saw these aliens but were all aware of their cataclysmic arrival. Weather systems had been profoundly disrupted and a torrential deluge inundated large segments of the earth. Nimbostratus clouds stripped the sun of its reassuring warmth and as one contemporary wrote: 'the sky's former incandescence was stifled by a rich and funereal grey'. The atmosphere was suffused with a terrible air of foreboding.

While most of us did not see these aliens, apparently we did in fact hear them. Presumably with the aid of some marvellous technological instrument, they managed to speak to us all telepathically in our own languages, be it vernacular Arabic or Zimbabwean Xhosa. Unfortunately, by what technological advancement or extraordinary feat of biological engineering they managed to achieve this we have no idea, given that we are now at the bottom end of the intergalactic caste system of 'unintelligent life'. Knowledge such as this is only privy to or understood by intelligent life forms as recognised by the Interplanetary Intelligence Index.

There are only a few remaining survivors left who are around to recall the horrendous event. However, they have all attested to the extremely unpleasant nature of telepathic communication. One survivor has described it as akin to having one's brain 'scraped inside out with a rake'.

The spokesperson for this diverse congregation of alien life forms was a being named Ra'Ghuz. In a speech that has been recorded and passed down from one suffering generation to the next, Ra'Ghuz explained to us, cooly and matter-of-factly, the motivation behind their unexpected visit. For the benefit of future generations and given the current danger to the few surviving written records we have, I have taken the trouble to render it again here:

> Creatures of Planet Earth. My name is Ra'Ghuz. I am Secretary-General of the Integrated Union of Intergalactic Civilisations. We are a trans-alietarian body dedicated to upholding the universal rights, prerogatives and values of all intelligent life. In defending these values we guarantee the peace, security and dignity of all civilisations.
>
> A space probe from this star system was intercepted recently by one of our members. A complaint was filed and we are here to investigate a very serious allegation. According to protocol and to prevent evidence tampering

> we cannot reveal the contents of this allegation. For the next three moon cycles we will be among you, collecting relevant evidence and witnesses. You will not see or hear us from this point forth until, on the appointed day, charges will or will not be brought. If charged and found guilty, our response will be swift and dramatic.

A rictus of dread paralysed the anxious face of humanity. What terrible, unequivocal words! A period of collective soul-searching, followed by riotous recrimination, took place. Accusations sprung forth and multiplied like maleficent cancer as we sought to hurl blame on anyone we could find. Families, groups and whole communities were ripped apart in this feast of internecine squabbling. Such is the *modus operandi* of panic.

Who and what was to blame? The International Space Station of course, and its arrogant crew of savants - how dare they put our future at risk, shooting random bits of junk into space. No! It was the Chinese gunpowder we had put on board. The IUIC had interpreted this artefact unfavourably, viewing us as a belligerent and murderous species. No! It was Autobahn by Kraftwerk, with its crushingly dull synths and lack of clear and sensible lyrical exposition.

No one for a second believed it could be Max Miller's sacrosanct novel.

As for the aliens themselves, as became clear later, they were shocked by what they witnessed on planet earth. They saw that a cult of personality had gripped the human population and that all sorts of strange and esoteric rituals were performed in the name of one man. They saw how his face adorned the wall of every house and home, how animals were sacrificed in his name, and how (almost) no one spoke ill of him. He was considered a saviour by all who uttered his name.

However, what the members of the IUIC found most baffling was humanity's frenzied and hysterical response to Ra'Ghuz's critical announcement. They had expected a more organised response from the accused, who rather than form a united council, began turning on each other and igniting fires. They noticed a marked behavioural difference in the response of human beings to their intervention and all the other surviving animals that populated the planet. We didn't know at the time that Ra'Ghuz's announcement was not only communicated to us telepathically but the animal kingdom as well in whatever form of sound, or units of expression, they had. When Ra'Ghuz had addressed us as 'creatures of planet earth' he had literally meant *all creatures,* not just us. It is possible humpback whales and various primates had the sophistication to understand at least certain fragments of the announcement. We know that some animals could indeed grasp and utilise concepts such as 'evidence' and 'complaint'. The complaint had launched an investigation that in its extreme infancy, did not identify one species as a culprit. We can only assume that we too, as unintelligent as we now know we are, only understood a diluted version of Ra'Ghuz's message.

And yet - call it a guilty conscience, or our anthropomorphic bias - we responded in a way that implicated ourselves. Whales and primates merely continued about their business, as if nothing had happened, keen to nurture what was left of planet earth. The IUIC wondered at their radically differing response. Either the animal kingdom was stoical by nature, had not understood or knew intrinsically that whatever had happened and caused these cataclysmic alien landings, it must be something to do with those damned human beings again. We have records attesting to dogs leaving their masters after decades of loyalty, clearly sensing the cardinal shift in the power dynamic. That is not to say they understood Ra'ghuz's message intellectually, but that they had intuited a profound change. For the entire animal kingdom this was an opening - a chance to be free of this domineering, parasitically reckless species. It is hard not to believe that on some fundamental instinctual level, they sensed a chance to return to a golden era, free of inverted food chains and slave labour. They could return to the buoyant chime of nature's watch and not the ruthless, mechanical ticking of food quotas, experiment, and annual slaughter. And so our companions, anticipating our reckoning, left us to shiver and stammer in the cold.

Max Miller - who had previously been making speeches, and giving lengthy public readings of his novel on a full-time basis - became conspicuously absent during these three months of anguish. Strangely enough, at first no one seemed to notice the lack of his presence. They were too involved with their own squabbles and the complete disintegration of the previous social order. But towards the end of the third month, as the impending day of judgement loomed ever closer, people began asking questions. Where was he in their hour of need? And how is it they had forgotten him so quickly? Were we really so fickle?

And then, the day of judgement finally came.

The day was the 2nd of October, a Friday, 2076. As with all days of unbearable consequence and resolution, the earth was wrapped in a stony silence. A universal shiver danced its way down the spine of humanity as our breath faltered under a chilly blanket of dread. There were no recriminations, no burnings and no looting on that day. There was only the pathetic gasp of a leviathan looking in the mirror for the first time and realising that her whole life, she had only been a mouse.

Ra'Ghuz's words are well known.

> Creatures of Planet Earth. We have made our assessment and charges have been brought. We find the following:
>
> Of the organisms inhabiting planet earth, we believe the human race and solely the human race is the guilty party.
>
> Of all charges every member of the human race is accused.
>
> Of all members of the human race, we suspect one member in particular to be guilty of especially serious and grievous crimes.
>
> This member of your species, who we believe you have aided and abetted in the most offensive way, will be brought to trial forthwith. The defendant shall be given a fair trial in the presence of witnesses. If the defendant is found guilty, your species shall be found guilty with it, and a sentence shall be passed.

I won't patronise my readers by telling them who this individual was.

It is here I would like to introduce the most crucial and valuable piece of history we have left - the entire centrepiece of this document. It has been the primary purpose of this record to provide the context for this vital source material, which taken on its own, might leave future generations confused. Thanks to a leak from the archives of the IUIC we have an almost complete account of the trial. The following is the only surviving extract from Max Miller's post-sentencing account, written by the very man himself.[20] As is made clear in the testimony, Max Miller wrote the account under duress, which might explain the somewhat flowery language contained within. Given that writing this account could have been Max Miller's last moment of freedom, it is not surprising he felt compelled to write in such extended and vivid detail.

To all those who read this, keep it protected and pass it on. Of our complex and vast history, this might be the only thing we have left.

—

Specimen 2, Max Miller, Post-sentencing Account

---

20. The following account the author presents us with, interestingly, was not meant for human eyes. Max Miller was legally bound to write a post-sentencing account of his experiences in accordance with Intergalactic Common Law. It was archived by the IUIC and was only smuggled out a few years later after presumably sympathetic insiders took pity on our rapidly diminishing history. At least, that's what we have been led to believe. As could be expected of a writer, the account is written like it is a piece of fiction. More disconcertingly, we have no proof this was actually written by Max Miller. We can only take it on faith.

October 2076 EY[21]

After Ra'Ghuz's proclamation I knew it was all up. Everything went black and a few days later I awoke submerged in a strange sponge-like compartment. I couldn't move and the gravity was strong. I found it hard to breath. I wasn't quite sure whether I was up or down – or whether those relative concepts even had any meaning. The first thing I noticed were thousands of continuous sucking motions over my whole body. I call it a 'compartment', but I couldn't help feeling however I was being contained by something alive. It was like I was being slowly digested in some gelatinous intestine, or conserved in an agitated jam.

I couldn't see. My eyes too were subject to the same sucking motions the rest of my body was. It is impossible to describe this feeling to someone who has not experienced it. Usually, an itch is something we feel happening to our body. But in this case I felt my body was happening to an itch. This physical sensation could only be described as utterly unbearable. I could not move to quench these ten thousand itches, happening simultaneously at different tempos across my entire person. The most infernal misery of all was the same irritation on the inside. My lungs, tonsils, eardrums, nasal passage, muscles and even bones caught no relief. I knew then that if I had been able to move and scratch myself, I would have torn every inch of flesh from my body and clawed myself to death. I coped with dreams of pain, and more humane forms of torture. I remembered lovingly the agony of a burn and the soreness of a wound. Anything but this infinite, ceaseless fucking itching!

And then there was the sound.

---

21. Earth Years.

I didn't notice it at first – driven mad by the immediacy of this agonising physical sensation. But soon I heard what sounded like thousands of little voices. They were screeches, some disgusting combination of squelching and aliveness. These suckers were like creatures, each squealing its own individual hymn of relentless suction. Dynamics and tone – loud and quiet, shrill and soft – became beloved memories. All my life I had not once given a thought to God, but then I asked him, without question of his existence, to make me deaf forever. I tried to scream, but no sound came out. The entirety of my mouth and throat was tortured by the same double-sided excruciation.

These suckers, consuming my body, never relented in their intensity, and neither did the associated sensations. After begging for God, I begged for madness – let my brain shrivel and eat itself, just like those damned Minnivih I had to go and write about. Anything but this! The more I begged for insanity, the more sanely aware of the physical suffering I felt.

After what could have been hours, days or months in this state my prayers were finally answered. But not by God.

At some indefinite point in time during these limitless hours of torture I suddenly felt a change in the gravitational pressure on my body. My breathing became even more difficult, as I realised I was being sucked, at some unprecedented speed, through some sort of mucilaginous tube. I was hurled – or spat out – onto a solid but bouncy surface. I bounced for some time until I reached equilibrium and found myself lying on the floor, covered in an offensive sludge.

The relief I felt was unimaginable, as if I had reached the gates of heaven itself. It didn't matter that I faced trial by the universe, awaiting a terrible fate or that I was covered in gunk, in some strange alien-crafted seal. I was free of the itching and those first precious seconds were the sweetest I had ever had in my entire life. But I couldn't relish my new freedom for long. Soon, I was met by the first alien life form I had ever encountered.

A sound of gas began filling the room and I found myself smelling a sweet-scented substance, not unlike perfume. Then it became visible. What I found appearing before me was not quite a solid, liquid or gas. Whatever scientific knowledge I had been equipped with was not fit for purpose to describe whatever substance I was looking at. I can only describe it as an amorphous translucent 'something'. I knew that it was life, because of the purposeful grace with which it moved. It did not have a face or a body - something in between. I felt that I in some sense knew it and looked at it. I felt it knew me too and looked at me, though it had no eyes with which to look. I wish I could describe with the limits of human language this extraordinary life form. What a shame our language evolved to suit such profoundly limited sub-regions of space. It is for this reason I think only people of profound spirituality could possibly comprehend the novelty of what I was apprehending.

'Hello, Max Miller.'

Just like Ra'Ghuz I was being spoken with telepathically, causing an uncomfortable, stabbing sensation inside my brain.

'Where am I? Who are you?'

The gaseous creature came right up close to my face. I could see inside its whole frame. Bits of it would occasionally flare into corporeal existence - a piece of flesh here, a bone there. Chunks of molecules in its body must have been continuously rearranging themselves; now a gas, now a liquid, now a solid, now…something else entirely. I had momentary glimpses of what it must look like in solid form, but these were so slight and sporadic that I could not form any definite picture. I sat mesmerised as all the parts of its being shifted its mode of existence like a shuffling, schizophrenic rubrics cube.

'You are in the Reduced-Capacity Custody Pen. I do not have a name. At least, not in the sense you mean. But I do have an identity, although it would be too difficult for you to understand. We do not use names – that is, four-dimensional language tokens.'

'Ra'Ghuz has a name,' I protested.

'Ra'Ghuz does not have a "name" like you mean – it gave itself a temporary four-dimensional language token in order to make itself memorable to your species. We do not need signifiers to communicate with each other.'

Each time I asked a question, I hesitated, knowing that the response would create the same unpleasant scraping sensation in my brain. The alien had completely stopped moving now and I felt that its frame was staring at me both expectantly and intently. This feeling combined with the snarky, condescending manner in which he spoke made me unusually quick tempered.

'Fuck you. I'm calling you Walter. You sound like a Walter.'

I began biting my nails, wondering which question was most important to ask. I had to keep its responses to a minimum if I wanted to avoid the resulting pain. Jesus, what I wouldn't have given to be back sitting on my cosy throne on planet earth. I missed worship. And constant praise. And biscuits.

It turns out he had already read my mind.

'Do not worry about the pain, it is not structurally damaging.'

Well, thanks a lot – I remember thinking clearly to myself.

'I understand you are frustrated.'

'Walter. Who is "we"? Why am I here? And what the hell is a Reduced-Capacity Custody Pen?'

Walter paused, which seemed odd, considering he could already read my mind before I spoke.

'"We" refers to all intelligent life. You are here because you are awaiting trial, and it is about to begin. The Reduced-Capacity Custody Pen, galaxy GN-z11, P-12, is a pre-trial detention zone for life of reduced mental capacity.'

'Reduced…reduced mental capacity?' I stuttered. This really takes the cake, I remember thinking. 'I'm perfectly sane!'

'You don't understand,' said Walter, 'by your own standards of analysis, you are "sane", as you put it. What I mean is that you are a member of a life form with an extremely low baseline of cognitive ability. It is, as a matter of fact, a great strain speaking to you, as I translate from our own methods of communication to an extremely restricted language system.'

I thought in relation to Walter, at that moment, in some very restricted, four-dimensional, expletive terms.

'Don't be upset,' said Walter. 'For you, this is a good thing. All of you, by default, if found guilty, will probably be sentenced on the grounds of diminished responsibility. In fact, you are very lucky to be even considered life at all – otherwise you would all have been exterminated and used for fuel already. It was only very recently we passed the Accreditation to Carbon Life Act, which granted living status to all carbon-based organic material.'

'That's awfully kind of you,' I said, slumping dejectedly.

I sat for a while, thinking of all those naive evolutionary biologists and their thoroughly limited scope. It turns out, DNA had only attained life status last year! Or somewhere thereabouts. I finally realised what it must be like to be a dog – where communication with human beings was indeed possible but limited – all the time dimly aware that in the background, some arcane apparatus of meaning ruled a domain of relations far beyond its understanding. I saw human perception and cognition for what it really was: a very special case of blindness.

I said nothing more to Walter for a while, as I let my brain recover from the lingering stinging sensation the conversation had left me with. This stinging sensation was at least nothing like the hell I had experienced just 15 minutes previously, where I had been practically tickled to death for weeks or months. To be honest, neither 'tickle' or 'itch' or 'pain' are words which adequately convey the feeling I had experienced in that terrible chamber. It had been like being stabbed and fondled by 10,000 feather-lined razors, and I was still reeling from the memory of it. I would rather die countless times than go through that again. Walter read my apprehension.

'Max Miller, if you are found guilty, it will be much worse than that.'

I shuddered.

'Tell me Walter. How long was I in that…thing for? And how is it I am still alive after so long without food or water?'

'You were only in there for 15 minutes,' replied Walter in a tone I took for nonchalance. 'In your time,' he hastily added.

'You were in a P-12 maintenance chamber. Properly speaking, the word maintenance chamber is somewhat misleading, because those chambers are in fact the living cells of even larger organisms called Hemoliths. P-12, where we are now, is a planet surrounded by these huge creatures. In each one we now support court and detention facilities. The cells – one of which you were in – are themselves composed of thousands of tiny creatures which absorb and recycle your energy back into you. This means that life forms who need to be in there for a long time – centuries, for instance – can stay alive and be maintained in excellent physical health. [22]

What was left of my psychological resilience had collapsed into a state of devastated enervation.

'Fifteen minutes?!' I gasped. 'I felt like I had been there for months! That is the most violent, intrusive and unbearable sensation I have ever experienced!'

---

22. The planet P-12 has now fallen into disuse, and is no longer used as a detention facility.

'Oh no. Our transition to using Hemoliths as detention facilities has been one of our most trans-alietarian innovations. We recently reformed the detention system after a class action suit by a number of life forms, which is why we transferred all our previous facilities to P-12. There is a consensus now that pre-trial detention shouldn't be cruel but the very opposite. It should be as pleasant as possible. After all, some of you may not be guilty.'

'So where are we now?' I asked in despair.

'In the waiting room.'

I felt a grim sinking feeling in the pit of my stomach. My eyes felt dry and I realised that I hadn't blinked for some time.

'Am I…are we…still in a "Hemolith"?'

'Yes,' said Walter. 'It's a waiting room, but technically we are just in another living cell. We're not that far from your maintenance chamber. You were transported here by an arterial vein. Aren't they wonderful? Hemoliths are one of the few organisms in the universe we have found that can contain nearly all forms of accredited life.'

I felt miserable now. The more it became clear to me I wasn't in a dream, the faster the tears swam down my face. I was utterly and truly alone. Except this time, not just psychologically. I had always felt lonely enough on planet earth, with my assorted group of correctly chosen friends. True, I could have had real friends, but I knew the path I wanted to tread. I cast aside thoughts of companionship, of a third husband, of love. As for my parents? Well, I had never been close to them anyway. I shed them as easily as a snake sheds its skin. The possibility of greatness had dwarfed everything else. By the time my online novel had been published, and I had changed the world, I reaped the rewards of my sacrifice. My ambitions were realised. And I will be honest with you. At the time, it was worth it.

I was worshipped like a God and slept the sweet dreams of a man whose legacy extended triumphantly and indefinitely before him. I had done the impossible. I, Max Miller, had defeated the internet, social media and its associated evils. The demagoguery of influencers, the scours of cancellation and the cultural illiteracy of our times would become a thing of the past. Never again would there be inane videos of cats, online spats about World War 2 or never-ending archives of abusive virtual porn. The tyranny of 'likes' and 'subscribers' would no longer be the benzine of a brutal social hierarchy. I had dreamed the impossible but it had begun to become true: we would return to more natural forms of entertainment, communication and physical contact. We would become Homo sapiens once again! Not digital packets of data, but dripping trunks of flesh and blood. When the internet had been put in its rightful place, as a store of information, rather than the medium through which we existed, society was brought to its senses. There was no religion or ideology left but one: the religion of ME.[23]

I had rendered the people stupid and made them children in my own image, as they returned to old forms of barbarism - constitutions, central government, culture. Society had seen me for who I was: a lean Beowulf who had slain a bloated Grendel. And like the warriors of Heirot, the people of planet earth sang my name. We didn't need social media to co-ordinate our behaviour and coexist peacefully. So long as every living human being worshipped me, peace would continue. I alone would be the consoling glue for a traumatised

---

23. There is some debate about this passage. Was Max Miller a visionary or just an extreme luddite?

civilisation. I would assuage this trauma and fill this confused chasm that I myself had created. This, my friends, was my genius!

As a living deity, in many ways, I was even lonelier than before. For the human race I was no longer an equal, or even a relation. I was an object, but an object of immense reverence and indefinable greatness. The absinthe of power had overwhelmed me with an addiction that numbed my emptiness and I wouldn't have swapped it for anything – not even the most delicate and intimate manifestation of tender human love.

Where were they now? My followers? My people? My ignorant, lovely children? I had left them all fatherless, and because of me they would now suffer the consequences. And now, I was even more lonely than before: GN-z11 was pretty much as far away from the Milky Way as one could go. I was in a context where I was seen as a blip of organic mass, barely worth the definition of life. And soon my fate would be decided by beings I could never hope to understand.

But what had I done?

Why was I on trial?

In my despair, I sobbed again and only stopped when I remembered that Walter had been reading my thoughts the whole time.

'You, Max Miller, are about to find out.'

Here, unfortunately, a small chunk of the account is missing. In the next passage we have 'Walter' and Max Miller engaging in discussion about the nature of the trial. Why a few paragraphs are missing is open to debate but given the otherwise full and intact nature of the account, I personally believe that information was contained in these paragraphs that were deemed too sensitive to leak.

'But this is ridiculous!' I cried. 'What do you mean I am to have no legal representation? I want a lawyer now!'

'A lawyer Max Miller? The institution of "lawyering" hasn't existed for millions of years. It is an ancient and out-dated concept – even a "dirty word", in your way of putting things. You see, adversarial systems of law are considered to be one of the most prominent signs of a retarded civilisation.[24] We have seen how courts like yours operate, with its polemic tennis of back-and-forth, between careerists trained to persuade and deceive. They are sources of entertainment, not excursions into the nature of truth. Lawyering is the technical study and application of sophistry, an elite form of storytelling. If the agenda is prescribed first – to acquit a client, or to find him guilty – then "the truth" is always reached from an incorrigible position of bias. Can you imagine if this was how science worked?'

I paused for a moment. That was in fact, pretty much, how science worked.

'So, I will be defending myself.'

Walter remained silent, which I took for affirmation.

---

24. This is vital and crucial evidence regarding the mode of pre-contact existence. It seems that during Reconstruction, when law returned as an institution, an adversarial as opposed to an inquisitorial system of law was instituted.

Suddenly, a strange vibration permeated the surfaces of the chamber. Aware that I was inhabiting something alive, I wondered if some internal biological process was the cause of the rumbling.

'Ah,' said Walter. 'That is the bell. It's time. I'm to accompany you.'

With my heart in my mouth, I looked expectantly at Walter. Accustomed to earthly logic as I was, I half expected him to take me by my hand and lead me through a maze of corridors to the court room. But of course, this was not what happened. I was to continue my initiation into the unsettling new precedent of suction.

Just as before, I was sucked through an arterial tube and discharged like redundant spit onto an unknown surface. When I landed it hurt like hell. There was no bouncing to equilibrium this time. I hit the floor with singular and painful finality. The first thing I saw was Walter beside me, his modes of form flashing and flickering its psychotic disco of existence. I closed my eyes, and sought God once again. I kept them closed for as long as I could. When I opened them, I was met with a scene so ineffable – so insane – I shrieked the shriek of a lost and condemned man finding himself to be in the heart of a new, unfathomable wilderness.

'Welcome,' said Walter, 'to the belly of the Hemolith.'

I stood on the edge of a vast extended platform, itself suspended across a black emptiness of seemingly bottomless magnitude. The platform on which I stood was red, slippery and thin, as if I was perched on the uvula of an ancient, frozen tonsil. All I could do then was stare into this darkness underneath, drenched in terrible silence. As my senses drowned in the reticent anonymity below, I dared not look above, behind or to my side. Shadowy hints at the edge of my vision whispered widths, lengths and depths of terrifying extension. I dreaded what shapes, what atrocities of non-Euclidean savagery, awaited me. I sought God for a third and final time and begged him for mercy. I begged for the dream to dissolve and the insanity to end. But most of all, I begged for context – a leaf, a drop of water, a grain of sand – anything that could remind me of planet earth and its attachments. I remained, with my eyes closed in this way, for some time. God was nowhere to be seen. This was divine retribution, I was without a doubt, and desert was about to be served up for the vain depredation of his identity.

I dared my eyes open again and looked straight ahead. After the appropriate registered shock, I looked to my sides as well. I still wasn't ready to contemplate 'the above'.

As far as I could tell I was in some sort of voluminous oviform structure. My brain acknowledged and sustained valid objections from my stomach, complaining of sickness and distress. Where I stood, in the centre of this vessel, I was equidistant from four distant concave surfaces; meaty, heaving walls of flesh beating some unknown rhythm to a far-flung biological clock. They seemed so far away I wasn't quite sure what I was looking at. Occasionally I thought I could see cascading blood pouring down its sides. The more I looked, the more I saw and now I caught glimpses of trawling veins, intermingling and nourishing not just a biological system, but the newly established courts and detention cells of the IUIC's justice system. It was presumably a vein like these that had projected me here.

I looked at Walter anxiously, now an anchor for me, having been only a few seconds before the very emblem of 'otherness'.

'W…Walter,' I stuttered. 'I don't want to look.'

'Stay calm,' Walter said, with a tone so unreassuring, even the most robust rock would have questioned its own solidity. 'Look,' he said solemnly, 'Look down below, and see who have come to watch your trial.'

At that moment, from Walter's inchoate form extended what resembled a hand, holding within it, a stone that shone as bright as the sun. Suddenly, the beneath I had taken for emptiness, was illuminated before me. The four surfaces I have just described, extended indefinitely below, adorned with thousands and thousands of pulpy platforms, populated with strange moving entities, which I do not have the facility to describe. Of various shapes and sizes, they squirmed and quivered in the distance.

'Thousands of members of the Integrated Union of Intergalactic Civilisations, have come to witness your judgement. Your case is something of a cause célèbre.'

I will gloss over the peculiarity of being spoken to in idiomatic French by a foreign alien life-form. At the time I was far too engrossed with the scene I was witnessing before me. As I looked down into the thousands of forms and lights underneath, I began to see the situation for what it was. I was the protagonist in a colossal, living theatre, with a populous audience seething with anticipation and observing my every move.

'Can they hear me?' I asked tenuously.

'They can hear everything.'

Small lights dotted the platforms below – multitudinous, piercing lanterns in the darkness – all staring up at me, expectantly. With a shudder of lucidity, I recognised them for eyes. I looked past these platforms, looking further into the depths beneath. At the horizon of my vision, where I could see platforms of teeming movement no longer, I could still see a distant, secret blackness at the centre.

'What is that? That point that I can't see?'

'There lie the intestines. If you're found guilty, you will be processed through those channels.'

I began to see why the Hemolith was such an attractive proposition for the IUIC. It was a massive digestive system, both literally and metaphorically.

'Do you know how much they paid to get here?'

A sinister question.

'Only one ticket was issued to each accredited civilisation. Staring up at you now are the eyes of 27, 631 representatives of every known civilisation, including my one.'

'Why are they so small?'

A strange sensation fizzled across the charred cortices of my brain. I now know that this was his way of laughing.

'Most of them are much bigger than you! You are looking at an array of lifeforms extending for some 3000 earth miles.'

At that point in time, for the first time in my life, I let out a noise not quite human. It echoed frantically forward, catapulting into the shimmering chaos, declaring to all present, the scream of the damned.

I collapsed onto my back, my eyes closed. I knew I was reaching the critical moment. From everything Walter had said, I knew that the punishment that could await me would be of tremendous proportions. My life flashed before my eyes, and I beheld it in full for one last timeless, prelapsarian second. I remember what I thought. Where are you now Augustine? With your infinitely small fragments of time? Where is its infinite divisibility when I need it the most?

Lord give me judgement – but not yet!

At last, as I opened my eyes and looked up, I saw the silhouette of a spheroid shape float towards me from far above. Soaked in the bright lighted eyes of the universe underneath, by the steady and inexorable tempo of its progress, I did not need telling who or what was approaching: my judge was coming. All I could do was stare and tremble. Unrecognisable sounds – foreign, telepathic squeals of joy – perforated my brain from outside. I did not need Walter to translate – a choir of cheers and whoops vibrated in the depths. It floated closer and closer towards me, come to judge a desperate man and placate a salacious audience.

The closer it came, I started to distinguish the features of this unknown floating thing. What I had taken for a sphere, was in fact a sphere of many spheres – small circular balls bound together in a circular shape. Then I noticed that these small balls or spheres – there must have been two hundred of them – were flashing, on and off, like a tight battalion of flicking, discombobulated light bulbs. Dots of black flashed everywhere across its face in configurations never the same as the one preceding it. That's what it looked like for a second or two: one giant speckling face. But to my horror, I realised that these were not anything like light bulbs, but fleshy eyeballs, each blinking its own idiosyncratic rhythm. The dots were blinks and the spheres glutinous eyes, proclaiming their viscosity in variously sized, grotesque form.

'Each of those eyes,' said Walter, 'is a different eye extracted from members of 250 of our most intelligent and illustrious civilisations. They are bound together by one central nervous system – a brain, if you like. They see and feel all that is to be seen and felt. He alone presides over every case brought to the Intergalactic Courts of Trans-Stellar Justice. He is simply known as 'The Judge'.'

Finally the object, or thing, or being, came within ten meters of my startled face. I saw that what Walter had said must have had some semblance of truth. Each eye was remarkably different, telling its own story of peculiar biological intricacy. Some were large, white and veiny, not unlike human eyes. Others wore patterns and features of obscure, evolutionary dynasties I could never possibly hope to understand. For these more obscure objects it was only their uninterrupted blinking that gave away their retinal nature. I couldn't help being fascinated by this creature. If I hadn't been in such a compromised position, I would have stared at it for as long as I could, asking Walter questions about its history, its structure, and exactly what 'kind of thing' it was. With all things of a dangerous and gruesome nature, one is repelled nearly as much as one wants to keep looking at it. Like a person enthralled by the enigma of a hideous spider – riveted to the spot and despite all attempts, unable to avert his gaze – I kept staring and staring.

The object of my curiosity suddenly stopped about 100 meters from my face. Or maybe it was a mile, or ten miles. I'm not sure. My judgement of size and distance was clearly erroneous, as Walter had made clear. My earthly brain wasn't used to expansiveness of such proportions. Immediately the cheering stopped and an expectant silence pervaded the belly of the beast. I turned my head circumspectly, only to realise, Walter had disappeared.

Suddenly, I felt a bell-like ringing lacerate my brain and pierce my ears. And yet - bell-like though it was - these high-pitched sounds somehow crashed and chaffed together, forming the unmistakeable coherence of words.

This is Court Clerk Trheyhzer. Case no. 33960495. Let the proceedings commence. Before us we have the defendant, one Max Miller, Specimen 2, Homo sapiens and representative of the human species by default. Given the inter-planetary and extra-jurisdictional complexity and nature of this case the trial shall operate in accordance with the Inter-regional Code of Tribunals. Sentencing guidelines shall also be followed according to those statutes. The defendant shall make a brief opening statement. Following this the complainant shall be called and make its case. The defendant shall be allowed to respond, following which, witnesses shall be called upon and brought forward. The Judge, in his perceptive omniscience, shall weigh up the relevant factors - the psychological and neurological state of the accused, his physiological response to the proceedings, an analysis of his thought content and a deep-memory brain scan for relevant historical and contextual factors. The credibility of the witnesses shall be determined in the same way.

There are two important elements in this case, that by constitutional decree, form important considerations:

According to Statute 7 of the Inter-regional Code of Tribunals, if the defendant, Max Miller, is found guilty of the charges, the human race shall also be sentenced accordingly. There is no precedent, as yet, of foreign lifeforms committing galactic-wide crimes, without the knowledge, abetting and condoning of its own species.

In so far as the accused acted in his own capacity as an individual agent, if found guilty, he shall be punished more severely than his species, which shall be given a lesser sentence according to these mitigating factors.

If the defendant is found guilty, he shall be immediately processed through the intestinal tract and transported to a maintenance chamber, where he shall be nourished and maintained for 500 years, in hemelian time, while the punishment chamber is prepared to specifications deemed appropriate to the crime.

Fuck!

I was beyond weeping now – my punctured emotional plumbing had leaked its salty all and my well of tears was truly exhausted. My neurological state? My physiological response? Walter's words about The Judge 'seeing and feeling' echoed in my mind. A bleak corollary of the court clerk's hefty statement seemed to be that the Judge was not only able to read my thoughts but many other things too.

And what was that about 500 years in a maintenance chamber? How long were hemelian years? Followed by specifically appropriate punishment? I can't tell you the thoughts I had then – how desperate they were. I couldn't go back to that maintenance chamber – please let me die, anything but that! I needed a defence! I didn't even know what the charges were! And then Walter's disparaging words, decrying our barbaric adversarial court systems, haunted me again. That and the fact that everything I was just thinking - right then and there - was already being processed and interpreted by The Judge. I hated this feeling of being read and felt - of being this collection of sense-data to be scrutinised, analysed and judged. There was nothing I could hide - not even this self-sufficient, immediate, singular thought, happening right now. I thought of all those human beings who had suffered so much in the Greasing Fields. I thought of all of them with a new empathy and solidarity.

Man. The price they had paid.

If the court clerk's voice had boomed and Walter's had condescended, the Judge's mode of speaking was more like an ensemble of whispers. Two hundred and fifty dangerous whispers.

'*Max Miller. I hope you have understood the structural procedure of this trial. We feel it necessary to make understood to you that great pains have been taken to speak and make ourselves intelligible in your form of language. It has been an intensive and neurologically expensive exercise. That said, we believe we have understood and equipped ourselves with the totality of your Earth languages satisfactorily. We would like to make clear to you that we will judge you fairly and appropriately. Of 33960494 cases we have processed so far over the last 6.7 billion years, no convictions have ever been appealed or overturned. With regards to our efficiency and accuracy, we believe this statistic speaks for itself. Before we begin, would you like to ask any questions?*'

'*Yes!' I found myself blurting out, speaking before I thought. 'If I am found guilty, what is the appeal process?*'

Aware that my life was in the balance, some remote survival drive had given fresh energy and purpose to my instincts. It was time to give myself over to more primeval technology.

'There is in fact, no appeal process.'

No wonder.

'Max Miller, would you like to begin with an opening statement.'

Being required to begin with a statement, against charges so far undisclosed, was like asking a blind swordsman to parry a blow. I straightened my back as hard as I could and tried to imbue myself with a sense of reverence. A feeling which did not come naturally to me.

'Mr. Judge. Sir. I do not know what the charges are. I don't know why no one has told me. There are however a few things I would like you and the audience to know. I have never harmed a man, woman, child or anyone else for that matter. I lived a life on earth that I would consider dignified and honourable. I strove to improve the lives of my fellows. I strove to improve our moral condition. I would even go as far to say I fought the most sinister modes of oppression. Sir. Mr. Judge. I cannot even imagine, for one damned instant, why you would consider me guilty of anything on planet earth, let alone the entire galactic system. In fact, I came to be respected and adored by my entire species for my work and my vision. I was an engineer of progress.'

Why was I speaking? He presumably had access to every neuronal firing and consequent thought before I even spoke. And yet, this felt the most appropriate way to respond. The sensation of the splutter, tinged with ridicule, that I felt vibrate across my brain, gave a strong indication of how the audience was taking all this. I had a queasy feeling that they all knew the charges too and that I was the only person in the entire cosmos who didn't.

'And what was the "work" you consider yourself to have carried out, Max Miller?'

A second splutter, like laughter, assaulted my senses. I had a dubious sense that everyone around me – all the spectators of the universe – were holding me in deep, sarcastic contempt. Who had known greater ignominy than this? Not even Monica Lewinsky, by my reckoning.[25] *To be laughed at, observed and criticised by the entire cosmos – not even the steamy backwaters of viral rumours, tabloid speculation and furious tweets could match this. I suspected that even The Judge was laughing at me somewhere beneath his veiny, glutinous exterior. On some metaphysical level, I had become a singularity – an infinitely dense, blackhole of shame and condemnation – sucking in the prurient gaze of the universe. No light could ever escape.*

'I'm not laughing Mr. Miller. This is a serious matter. Answer the question.'

I paused and scoured the inner recesses of my memory. Apart from some minor infidelities in my youth, I was sure there were no major skeletons in my closet. Well, there was that time I lost my virginity

---

25. American activist, 1973 - 2069. She came to public attention during the Clinton-Lewinsky scandal as a result of which she was unfairly demonised by the media and segments of the general public at the time. In the second half of the twenty-first century, in the aftermath of Max Miller's Great Gambit, she was revered as something of a saint. Her work denouncing cyberbullying was considered seminal in bringing to public awareness issues surrounding the internet, social media and its evolution.

with my first boyfriend – in that abandoned synagogue – when I was about fifteen. But God, or Yahweh, didn't exist anyway. Or so I had thought. What could I have done so terribly wrong? If God hadn't existed for me then, I was pretty damn sure he didn't exist now. Judging by the abundance of civilisation manifest right in front of me and beneath this icy podium, God (if he ever existed) had had far more ambitious projects in mind than the human race. Against a plethora of super-intelligent, telepathic beings, the thought struck me that the human race must have been either a haphazard first draft or a drunken accident. If you had boundless, accelerating space as your canvas, you can see how easy it would be to construct whatever drivel came to mind, discard it, and forget about it forever. Who knew how many beings and substances there were out there just like us – the discarded residue of God's creative process.

'My work…' I muttered hesitantly. I looked into the many eyes of The Judge, and projected onto them the most sincere expression I could muster.

'I rebelled against the poisonous fabric of society. I wrote a book. A novel. It was called The Plight of the Minnivih. It changed the world, and we put the beast of all our oppression – the internet – in its place. The novel was a grand metaphor. All I did was concern myself with the condition of the human race. I tried to elevate our consciousness. Have you any idea how barbaric human society was before? Do you know what malicious mechanisms we had constructed, and the impunity with which we all punished each other? Human society had started devouring itself – figuratively that is. Just like the brains of the Minnivih in my book. We had fallen into an abyss of inhumanity! I saw myself as a saviour – and I still maintain that is exactly what I was. How could you let all this bother any of you? We may not be the most peace-loving species, but the vicinity of our

misdemeanours was restricted to planet earth, the moon and a heap of trash left floating in our orbit. I didn't even know other civilisations existed! How could I have broken any trans-galactic law?'

'The book. You are claiming it was a metaphor?' asked The Judge with a tone I interpreted as incredulous.

'Yes! What else could it be?'

No laugher. No response of any kind. Just vigilant silence.

'Are you aware, Max Miller, of the space probe you call Voyager 3?'

My thoughts buzzed like ecstatic, coked-up flies. Voyager 3…Voyager 3…Voyager 3! I had completely forgotten about it! That stupid shuttle they had to send into space. I knew nothing good was going to come of that. I remember thinking at the time, back then, what a stupid idea it had been to provoke the universe. But in my vanity, I let it go.

I gulped.

'Yes, Mr. Judge, sir.'

'Do you wish to add anything else, before we consider your opening statement concluded?'

'No,' I said resolutely. I had been as honest as I could.

'Good. Bring forth the complainant!'

At last, I thought. I would finally find out what curmudgeonly fuck had taken issue with my harmless existence. But that thought itself,

I remembered, was being taken into consideration in all its nastiness and ill will. With regards to my thought processes, I tried my utmost to put system 1 in the back seat and put system 2 into driving mode. If I was to have any chance of making it through the trial safely there was no room for dangerous impulsive thoughts.

Thinking these things, against the now familiar hush of expectation, I heard a rapid, enthusiastic noise. Gushing out of the fleshy horizon, a tonsil-like podium, just like the one I was standing on, spurted forth. On its rounded tip, just some 20 meters away from me, stood an emaciated, slanted figure. It took me a while to distinguish its features but before anything else, I was struck by its beauty. I watched it as it stood, transfixed by the way it moved so delicately, so vulnerably – like a wilted flower, waving lithely to the insouciant winds of nature. Or shimmering grass, moving to invisible undulations.

As it came closer I saw something I hadn't seen for a very long time. A face – almost familiar! And what beauty and sadness it conveyed. It had two gleaming eyes, suffused with recent moisture. A mouth, not unlike a human's, was etched sadly into its sallow cheeks. Its expression, inhuman though it was, made no secret of its melancholy. Something inside me told me that this pathetic creature had resigned itself to a passive existence – a forlorn and injured receptacle of the feelings and actions of others. Yet despite this, I inwardly rejoiced to be once again with something intelligible and familiar. Its figure was hominid-like too, with lanky arms and legs. I felt a physiological and psychological rapport with this creature, despite its being my legal adversary. It was almost as if I had seen it somewhere before. What could I have possibly done to upset this shrivelled, fragile entity?

It was the court clerk first who took a chisel to the icy silence.

'Judge, defendant Max Miller and to all those present: we have before you, specimen 357, of the planet W-23. Would you state your name for the court and The Judge?'

'My name is Frieyhah.'

I took another good look at my accuser. It seemed a great shame something so beautiful could hold so much against me. Unlike the other life forms I had encountered, she spoke from her mouth. I wondered if this was a sign of lower intelligence, like mine apparently was. I couldn't be sure of its gender, but the voice was feminine, and not unlike a human's. I saw her as a 'she'.

'Please state your complaint.'

'As the intergalactic community is well aware, I am the member of a race that has been reduced to dwindling numbers. A great calamity struck my people, and it has been with your help that a few of us – refugees now – have managed to survive. My own daughter succumbed to this very disease herself and I live with the painful memory of her loss.'

My jaw dropped in astonishment. Part of me realised then and there where this was leading, but I dared not even admit it to myself. The thought I had then was so preposterous, its possibility so impossible, that I suppressed it as soon as it emerged. I looked again down below, at the thousands of flashing eyes, and felt queasy. I hadn't quite taken in that this obtrusive, cnidarian pulpit upon which I stood, was much narrower than I had assumed. If I moved so much as two steps, I would fall into the abyss. It was lucky that for all this time I had remained stone still, consumed by so many other daunting particulars. If I had fainted, that would have been it.

Judge. For those of us left, our existence is afflicted by the terrible legacy of this catastrophe. As all of you are aware, eight moon cycles ago, in our time, the objects contained in Voyager 3 were publicised and made accessible to all civilisations within the Integrated Union of Intergalactic Civilisations. Among the items on board Voyager 3 was Max Miller's book, The Plight of the Minnivih.

'We, the Minnivih, believe that the life form that stands before you, Max Miller, has added fresh salt to our wounds. In his book, which we have read as have many of you, Max Miller describes the very fate of my own daughter, Meiyhah, and the destruction of my people. Max Miller has taken the history not just of my daughter, but of my entire race. He has appropriated our history, our habits, our customs, and exploited it for entertainment. And to add insult to injury, he used our very demise – mechanising its poignancy for his own self-aggrandisement – to have himself slavishly worshipped as a God. Listen to me Max Miller. You are no original. You are no prophet. You are a crook and a pirate, and you have swindled our culture for your own gain. Curse you and your disgusting people, who drank your poison so thirstily!'

That transient fidget of a thought I had suppressed so violently shone before me in all its concrete legitimacy. The impossible was in fact possible. I was being told by the mother of a fictional character I had made up, that this race I had created from my very own imagination, did in fact exist. There was just no way! I felt as if I had been somehow set up.

'Let's reduce the hyperbole,' The Judge announced resolutely. While the majority of those 250 eyes maintained their line of sight fixed on my accuser, I noticed that at least a dozen of them were closed. I wondered if they were sleeping. I could see still others whose pupils

darted about spasmodically. Distracted perhaps? Or were they monitoring things I couldn't see?

Judge. I believe the defendant, Specimen 2, Max Miller, Homo sapiens, of planet earth, is guilty on two counts of cultural appropriation of the first degree – that is, of a pre-meditated nature and of malicious intent. I believe the human race, for disseminating Max Miller's book through their society, and praising it, are guilty of cultural appropriation on two counts of the second degree – that is, aiding Max Miller with the intention of malice and harm in the form of mockery to our species with deleterious consequences to our sense of dignity and identity.'

This had to be a set up! There was absolutely no way this was within the realms of human possibility. But then again, we weren't within the realms of 'human' possibility. I was now playing chess with scales of probabilities so unimaginably vast, my meagre conceptions of what was likely and what was not no longer bore any meaning. And yet, the idea that the intricate story and characters I had developed for my novel could in any way factually coincide, in all its detail, with an actual state of affairs seemed as unlikely as a monkey managing to type Shakespeare's Hamlet by randomly hitting keys on a typewriter. By any measure, surely the chances had to be so improbable, as to be absurd. This was exactly why I needed a defence. I needed time – to find out who was setting me up, and what sort of game had been so maliciously constructed against me.

The Judge, of course, had read my mind.

'You think you have been framed, Max Miller?'

Finally, the pressure was too much. I lost my head.

'Yes! I do!' I responded vociferously. 'She's lying! I demand to know who's the puppet master in this evil game! Who's paying who?! And who's paying her?! And what are you being paid in? Or do you even have payment as a concept? Agh! I don't know by what incentives your actions are guided, but for God's sake show me something MEANINGFUL. Show me something I can UNDERSTAND. Show me WHY and HOW! You don't tell me the charges! Then you state the impossible! And now I don't even know what you evil bastards…'

My mouth and brain froze mid-sentence. A telekinetic force – I don't know what else it could have been – had interrupted my tirade. I didn't need telling by whom.

'Max Miller. I understand your frustration. Clerk! It is time, I believe, we show you Max Miller – and the spectators – Exhibit 1.'

I was released from my paralysis and looked around expectantly. Nothing seemed to be happening. I had expected some third podium to spring out of the horizon, just like I and Freiyhah had, with an object conspicuously titled 'Exhibit 1'. But again, circumstances made a mockery of my earthly expectations.

'Show me wha…?'

Suddenly, my brain froze again. But this time my vision became obscured and I couldn't see. My hearing became muffled too and I felt as if I had been transported to some different place and time.

And indeed I was.

I cannot describe to whoever reads this, human or not, the apparition I saw and felt then. As I write from my chamber, it is all a blur to me now. The very apparition itself was dimensionless - the sharp edges of space and time all smudged into one. One moment, I was rocketing through galaxies near the speed of light, at another I found myself observing a small, purple planet from a distance. At still another, I saw before my very eyes the emaciated figures of life forms, scrawny and sluggish, doing strange things to themselves with their hands and faces. I realised immediately who they were. It was the Minnivih, in their last act of existence, raping and eating themselves to oblivion. And yet it was not like how I had imagined it in my novel. It was more real, more desperate and more disturbing. In those dimensionless moments I saw how they evolved, communicated, embraced. I saw each one of them, in their hundreds of thousands, all as individuals, all with their unique characteristics and quirks of personality. It was all true! They were all real! A thousand times more real than my book! In the timelessness of everything, I saw and got to know each of them one by one, with their separate lives and histories. Not just Freiyhah, and Meiyhah - who were real to me in my own sense of space and time - but the ones I had never, and would never meet; all the individuals I had approximated, and so vastly underestimated, in my novel. I longed to speak to them. I could see them in all their sincerity…

'End of Exhibit 1' grunted the court clerk.

Back in my four co-ordinate parametric system, I did that time, very almost faint. My knees began to wobble and were it not for the sudden appearance of Walter, who steadied me with a momentary flash of bodily substance, I would have definitely fallen. Fallen not just physically, I felt, but in other ways too.

'Have you anything to say in response Max Miller?'

'I'm…I'm sorry,' I stuttered, as I dropped to my knees.

I felt crushed by all the categories of sadness only someone who has had such an experience could understand. I felt as if I had been with them, and in knowing each of them – with all their hopes, dreams and potential – had suffered alongside them the many gauntlets of pain to which they had all been subjected; the pain I had so tactically written about, in my brilliant but misguided grab for power. I regretted it now, and yet I still couldn't believe it. I did feel sorry. I felt sorry for them – but more than anyone else – for myself. The waves of empathy I had been so overcome by soon turned into the sticky mud of boundless self-pity. I waded in it up to my neck, the dirty creature that I was, staring up into the deafening black of outstripped possibilities. I would never go back to planet earth. I would never see my home again. I would never share an intimate moment with another human being. Sinking deeper and deeper, the mud now up to my eyes, I looked on as all possible futures died their many unfulfilled deaths.

And yet, it is possible that at this point I still had some speck of hope – some atomic glisten of belief that I would still come out alright. What human wouldn't? Until the curtains snap violently shut, it is impossible not to believe the play will somehow go on. To be a mortal being is to live in violent contest against the impossibility of immortality. If we didn't, why would we ever get up in the morning? So long as we shove death into the distance, casually accepting it happens to others (but not us!) we can go on living our lives, constantly slapping thin layers of weak paint over the indestructible portrait of Death's face. Sometimes in moments of weakness, as the paint peals away, we see glimmers of it, peering through these counterfeit materials, as unchanged as it always was. So we apply another flimsy layer of pigmentation – whatever a business, idea or God will sell us – and sit with it for a while as comfortably as possible, for as long as we can. Even I, both a seller and a buyer in this fraudulent transaction between the living and the inevitable, was no exception. I still believed that there was a way out of this dire situation. It was then – not yet drowned and still optimistically pounding on the doors of my coffin lid – the final nail was fitted, screwed and bolted with the expert finish of Fate.

'Clerk! Please bring forward the one and only witness.'

What witness? The human race? My data cookies? I heard a familiar gushing sound and a third podium sprang forth. I don't know what I suspected but if I had truly appreciated the ironic tragedy of my situation I should have predicted it. I had longed for planet earth maybe just a little too readily. On that third podium was the one thing – or person – I least wanted, let alone expected, to see. As I recovered from the speed of her apparition and a mirage of surprise, I saw her in all her unmistakable likeness. It really was true. There she was!

That bitch – Valerie Craft.

I told myself to fight the visceral sensations of ill will percolating through my gut. The less control I had over my emotion the more The Judge could hold against me. He was 'feeling' everything – or so I had been told. The thought even crossed my mind that impossibly, somehow, my nemesis had brought about all these absurd circumstances herself. I even – dare I say it – cursed the female sex. I had been happy enough loving men – slightly imperfect extensions of myself. I had spent the last few years tackling oppression, so I thought, with the writing and dissemination of my novel. Now I saw the other side of the power imbalance. Oppression occurs for a very good reason. It keeps people like me alive.

'Judge, defendant Max Miller and to all those present: we have before you, specimen 1 of planet earth. Would you state your name for the court and The Judge?'

'My name is Valerie Craft.'

I had so far avoided looking at her, wishing not to engage the undoubtedly arrogant, look-at-you-now contortion of glee written across her face. Looking at her would be like admitting defeat or acknowledging my enemy, pathetic, vanquished adversary as I was becoming. But as her cold, scheming voice tuned its strings for the overture of condemnation surely on its way, I had to look up. I had to look at the woman who could just be on the verge of sending me irrevocably and crashingly down.

Her face was not like her virtual profile – not in the least. In her vofiles[26] she had always looked austere and very thin. Not the usual influencer type. I had to reluctantly admit to myself that she was very well turned out and looked the picture of health. Particularly for her age. Her cheeks were coloured with a lively, vibrant red and her fair hair lapped cheerfully down the fronts of her shoulders. There was one thing nevertheless that held true both to the rumours and what I had taken for a glitch in her online vofiles – she really did have a crooked neck, with her head slanting ever so slightly to the left. Yet this in no way seemed to efface her allure. She was wearing odd twentieth century looking clothes. A short black dress and a white

---

26. In the latter days of the internet short three or four second videos served as profile images for virtual persons.

shirt – a garment long since abandoned for its clear associations with white male capitalism. Given our relative positions and situations, I am sure she was scoffing at me down to her very clothing.

'Valerie Craft,' said the Judge, in its cerebral whisper of a voice, 'you volunteered yourself as a witness for this trial. While we don't usually accept witnesses from the same numbers of the accused, we believe that you must have had very good reason for doing so. It is not in your interest to implicate your own species. We believe this puts your testimony on an altogether different and higher footing. Before you give your testimony we must ask you a number of important questions.'

Valerie Craft waved a flexuous strand of hair from her face nonchalantly. I couldn't understand why she looked so damned comfortable. Had she not been through the same traumas I had, landing in the belly of the Hemolith? Undoubtedly she had not been subject to the miseries of the maintenance chamber. That and a phenomenal talent for embracing the uncanny.

'Yeaaah,' said Valerie Craft graciously, with her charming Texan lilt. 'Please go ahead.'

'Valerie Craft. Do you know Max Miller personally?'

'No sir.'

'Do you have any interest, outside of impartiality, that could have moved you to give testimony today?'

'No sir.'

Like hell she didn't!

'So why did you come forward today?'

Valerie Craft looked askance ruefully, performing what she clearly thought was an impassioned gesture of sincerity. She was, like me, a true virtuoso in the theatre of life.

'I have been a strong believer in justice from the day I came out of my mother's womb. I lived my life adhering to it and trying to enforce it where I could. In fact, before I was even a teenager, I gave up my very own parents to the law. What more proof of commitment to justice could there be than that?'

So it was true! If she was the type of person willing to turn in her own parents, she wouldn't bat an eyelid to snitch on the human race so long as it meant taking me down with them. She had always hated me so much. I knew that. I was a threat to her existence. But now I was facing malice of proportions and ambition beyond anything I had encountered before. If the Judge 'saw and felt' everything, how was he not objecting to this ill-fitting costume of honesty and good will? What about those 'deep-memory brain scans' the clerk mentioned at the start of the trial? I thought The Judge was supposed to know all our histories, our intentions and our thoughts. Or maybe he did really know all this and was allowing us to expose ourselves for the dissimulating, shit-conjuring animals that we are.

Judge!' I interjected. 'She tried to get me killed!'

Again my brain froze. My throat muscles were suspended mid-speech, forced into the silent quiescence demanded of an unpleasant, external force.

'You have had your opportunity to speak Max Miller. Valerie Craft. Is it true that Max Miller, who stands before us here, did indeed write the book, The Plight of the Minnivih? It was not written by someone else, using the name of Max Miller?'

'Yes, your honour, that is correct.'

'And you witnessed its publication and subsequent dissemination?'

'As much as such a thing can be witnessed, yes, that is correct.'

'Have you read The Plight of the Minnivh?'

'Yes sir, Judge sir, I have.'

'And what were your impressions of the book?'

'It's hard to know what I would have thought had I not already had some preconceptions. The book had become wildly popular by the time I forced myself to read it. I am a strong believer in the public and I approached it with the same reverence many others did at the time. But after even the very first few pages I felt a sick feeling in my stomach, that some grave wrong was being committed. I won't lie to you, some of the prose was excellent. But the content was… well…unsettling.'

'And what did you find unsettling, Valerie Craft?'

'Reading The Plight of the Minnivih was a bit like accidentally coming into the possession of someone else's wallet – a personal object containing an identity, a wealth, a history. This book, thing, novel,

whatever it was…I felt a peculiar obligation towards it. That it ought to be returned. But to whom to return it I did not know.'

'Returned? In what way, and why?'

Valerie Craft pretended to mull over the question. I knew, and she knew I knew, that she had planned every word and caesura of her speech to the very last detail. There was not one instant of her deliberate pauses for thought that hadn't been expertly pre-choreographed. That and her intoxicating Texan twang, emphasising the 'h' in every 'what' and 'why' – how could I not be captivated?

'In what way I did not know. But as to why…I felt confident that the content before me was in fact stolen.'

That duplicitous, lying…And again my thought processes were strangled. So The Judge could read what I thought?! I was certain it was him who held this miraculous power over my body.

'Had you ever had this feeling before?' asked The Judge.

It was then that Valerie Craft looked at me for the first time, swallowing me up in her delighted and decadent gaze. The pupils of her eyes laughed at me in all their corpulence. She was gobbling me piece by piece in this ecstatic dinner she had so carefully helped prepare and had served to her. Her turquoise eyes were so splendid I could not look away. They were treacherous snares of beauty. She was like a great dame from a 1960s Western. She even spoke like one.

'Yes. I had. My Ma and Pa were farmers. When I was a little girl I used to walk from the corn fields right up to the edge of a small enclosure surrounded by old barren trees. We used to call it

The Hedgehog – the way its branches stuck out so. It was understood that that was my private place, my special place to go. If I saw Ma or Pa, or a neighbour, get close to it I used to feel a combination of fear and rage, like maybe a mother would over a child. It was my space and my space only. My parents understood very well that if you want an obedient child, you had to give it free rein over some defined region of space, no matter how small. For some it's a doll house, for me it was The Hedgehog, and I used to go there to play all my imaginary games. No one went in the enclosure. Only I did. And when I wasn't there I watched over it from my bedroom. There was nothing special about the Hedgehog. Only that it was mine and that it was sacrosanct. Mine to protect.

'One day, it was late autumn – I remember – in those days we still used to notice the seasons changing – a terrible thing happened. I was walking and jumping to the centre of the enclosure as I always did when I woke up in the morning – that was my little way of reclaiming it from the moon and the stars – and I saw something small and brown on the ground. I saw that it was a teddy bear, muddy and dishevelled. It was hand-made and roughly sewn, which is a rarity of course. Everything on earth is factory made. As I rubbed the dirt from its tawny fur I appreciated the handwork that had gone into this beautiful toy. But it wasn't a toy! It was something personal and loved. Something that had belonged to someone. Every thread and button had been put together with the intentionality of a loving human mind and I could see by its chewed, bitten ears, it had been loved as such too. To someone this thing was real and alive, with a name and identity. I was overcome with shame. This beloved object was in my garden, right in the damn middle of it. I knew that I had come by something I shouldn't have. I knew that I wanted to do right by someone but I didn't know how. Anyway, I ran home crying madder than a wet hen. I told Ma and Pa I was a

good-for-nothin' thief. They told me I shouldn't cry, that it was mine now. Pa said – he still spoke old like –"darlin' you should keep it! You should keep it or you might could even sell it!" And it was then I saw the very first glimpse of who my parents really were: thieves and hustlers themselves through-and-through, without one bit of honesty. Reading Mr. Max Miller's book felt just a bit like that.'

'In what way?'

Valerie Craft flicked another wisp of hair from her face with an affected turn of the head.

'You know. Like I had something that wasn't my own. And that this thing that belonged to someone else…someone other else was trying to sell it.'

What a master! What a passionate auteur of sophistic sculptures of slime! And the story of the teddy bear. How long had it taken her to come up with that one? I had to respect her talent and her mastery over an act of revenge so dazzlingly constructed and performed. All that time she had been in the Greasing Fields, she must have had a lot of time to think. In her spare moments of recess and fantasy, wherever she had space for a free thought or dream, I'm sure she had welded my pretty face to a thousand savage fates. Amidst the quotidian drudgery of greasing machines, it was these reveries that must have lubricated and greased her own quaking organism. But of all those inspired and horrendously construed futures I'm sure not even she had predicted this one. And how delighted she must have been for her own wildest dreams to have been surpassed. Not only would she call for the sound of my death knell, she would ring the bell personally up on high in the presence of all the representatives of the universe. For an influencer like Valerie Craft this was attention beyond anything she could have hoped to have savoured on planet earth. This was her apotheosis. She was on the peak of peaks, from which there was no higher point to see or climb. Heaven was in sight for her and she could almost touch it. But like the Tower of Babel, I prayed she and her monolithic structure of deceit would all soon come crashing down.

As for me. Well, I was like a man whose only response left to an impossible jigsaw is to throw all the pieces in the air and laugh hysterically. There was no way of fitting these broken pieces together no matter what I did. I was a Dmitry Karamazov – events, people and profound coincidence had conspired against an innocent man flawlessly. Acquittal was impossible. She had cast me as the ultimate thief and of all the forms of larceny, I had committed the most atrocious. I had not stolen a material thing but something much more egregious – something intangible, symbolic, sacrosanct. I was a pilferer of innocence and identity. And worst of all not only had I stolen it, I had sold it.

Or so she said.

And yet, despite all this, there was still one thing I just couldn't figure out. I knew The Judge could read my mind. It couldn't have been anyone but The Judge who had frozen my thought processes at least two times now, apparently offended by the content of my thoughts. So why was he allowing this perjury to continue? Unless of course, Valerie Craft's story was true, but I couldn't believe that for one second. Valerie Craft did not hark to the orders of conscience and morality. This was clear to anyone who had witnessed her activities on planet earth. She was someone who hated to be dominated and needed to dominate herself. This was the real reason she had ruthlessly expunged her parents. Like she had said herself in her quaint little anecdote, she had wanted free rein, not over an enclosure, but over much, much more. She saw early on these desires would have been incompatible with her strict, evangelical parents.

I wished I could have been in a room with her. Just me and her – I'm not quite sure why. I don't know what I would have done or said. I wouldn't have assaulted her, that's for sure. That had never really been my style. I don't think it would have made me feel any better either. Her revenge was hermetically sealed. It was perfect. Complete. Impregnable. I could have killed her and it wouldn't have made any difference. And she knew this. But what I wouldn't have given to pick her fascinating brain. What had become of her after the Greasing Fields were abolished? By what artifice had she ended up on an alien witness stand on P-12? What sort of appalling plan had she hatched? But ultimately, these were all ancillary to the most beguiling and terrible question of all. Like an antichrist she had risen from the muck, despised and derelict, and realised her own bastardised salvation – a tonsillar, extraterrestrial podium from which she could strike a stake into the heart of humanity. How could she be so happy to destroy the very enablers who gave her life? Writing my statement, as I am now, I think I finally know the answer.

'Tell us Valerie Craft,' said The Judge. 'Tell us the effect Max Miller's book had after it was published. How did your kind respond to the book?'

'Well,' said Valerie Craft confidently, 'it was nothing short of a sensation. More than that. It was adored and worshipped like The Bible once had been.'

And it was here! At that moment the rains stopped and the clouds of despair parted ways like the Red Sea for the hand of Moses: Valerie

Craft had made her first fatal mistake. I could feel it in my bones. The witness cross-examination was about to commence.

'The Bible?'

I could tell by The Judge's tone and the way my brain sizzled that The Judge had genuinely no idea what Valerie Craft was talking about.

'Yes, your honour. It used to be the cornerstone of our society, some decades ago. It was a silly book about a man, who's also God – the One God – who's also his own father at the same time, who lets his son die – well, he's his father too, so he kind of lets himself die and… Excuse me.'

Valerie Craft hesitated, then coughed – one of those genuine fake coughs.

'Sorry, I'm mightily confused now myself. I used to understand this very well.'

I heard, or felt, a murmuring in the depths. The spectators were apparently becoming excited. The way my cortices were being fried, I could tell The Judge was excited too.

'So, if he was God, the one God, how could he have died? Can a God die?'

'No. God is omnipotent and eternal, sir. Well, supposed to be. According to this book.'

'And yet he died?'

'Killed, sir.'

'Who killed him?!'

'His, er…children, sir.'

'And why did he let himself be killed if he was omnipotent, and he can't actually die, if He was God?'

'He was in human form sir. He died in human form. He was flesh and blood – and something else, I think. He was a word.'

For the first time in the proceedings, I noticed Valerie Craft was beginning to become irrevocably unstuck. She had begun digging herself into a hole and so long as The Judge continued to explore his bewilderment she was compelled to keep digging.

'He was a word, Valerie Craft?'

'THE word, sir. Excuse me. THE word.'

'So this God, Valerie Craft, this omnipotent, eternal God, who was also the father of himself, and was killed by his children, and was actually a human, and not a God – but somehow still a God at the same time – was also this word?'

'Er. Sir. Um…Yes. Sir. Now you say it, I think that's right.'

'And what was this word? The word?'

The atmosphere in the court room – or rather, hemelian stomach chamber – was stifling. The tension was tangible.

'I…er…I don't know sir,' she croaked. She sounded on the verge of tears.

'So what happened after he was killed? Did planet earth change without the God?'

'Not exactly, Mr Judge. The world went on completely as normal. He was actually kind of still alive I guess.'

'So he was alive?'

'No, actually, I think he was dead. He was definitely dead.'

'So what is important about this story Valerie Craft? God died, and planet earth carried on as normal. Why was this story so important to your people?'

What had begun insidiously as an affected, thespian cough had turned into authentic, desperate spluttering.

'Well, sir, he rose up from the dead three days later.'

'He rose up? From the dead? Is it normal on planet earth for dead organisms to become reanimated?'

'No, sir, it's unheard of sir…that's why…'

Valerie Craft was rudely interrupted.

'Clerk Trheyhzer! Are you noting this down?'

'Yes Judge. This is all being recorded, Judge, for our archives.'

'Tell me, Trheyhzer, do we have any records in our archives of dead things becoming alive again?'

'No Judge. Otherwise they wouldn't be dead.'

It seemed clear to me at this point that the court proceedings had become completely derailed. If it hadn't been for The Judge himself, gorging his perplexity with questions of accretive incisiveness, I am certain issues of 'relevance' would have been called into question. What a relief it was, for the first time in my life, not to be the centre of attention.

'Are you lying to the court Valerie Craft?'

'No sir, I never lie, sir. It's just a book.'

'And yet you tell me this book had great influence, like Max Miller's novel allegedly had? What sort of influence did this book have?'

Valerie Craft scratched her head - a number of many subsequent gesticulations that hadn't been carefully choreographed.

'Well, sir, lots of people got killed, sir. For about two thousand years.'

The Judge paused for longer than usual. This super-intelligent being, who I imagined thought at speeds millions of times faster than human beings, was apparently thinking for a very long time.

'Valerie Craft. There's just one thing that really bothers me.'

'Yes, sir. Go ahead.'

'Who or what brought him back alive?'

'God, sir. God brought J…'

'He brought himself back alive?!'

'I guess so.'

'Are you getting this Treyhzer?'

I could see something odd was happening to The Judge, as its eyes darted around disconnectedly in all directions, from south to north-north-west.

'Is it possible to make yourself be again, if you no longer are? If he no longer was, how did he make himself be?'

'Well, his dad did it from heaven. You see, his son was on earth, but his dad was in heaven.'

'He was in two places at once? As well as being dead and alive at the same time? All that time being one God, or person, the father of himself?'

'Well, sir, he was actually three people…or Gods.'

'The one God was three Gods, who were also people?'

'No, no! He was three people or…how do I put it. He was two people and one other thing, that isn't really a thing, as well. Sorry. Not two people, that's wrong. Wait. I've got it. He was a God, a human being, and that other thing that isn't really a thing. He was those

three things. That's it. I'm sorry Mr. Judge! I used to know! I used to know all of this.'

When The Judge next spoke, it was clear some sort of judgement had been reached in his mind.

'Trheyhzer, do we have an intelligence score for the human race, as of yet?'

Trheyhzer's sycophantic, high-pitched voice, rang through my mind the more thunderously for not being able to see him.

'No Judge. The human race has not yet been assessed for intelligence.'

The Judge's many eyes had returned to a dull, almost sedated, equilibrium as if he was suddenly very bored. Whatever curiosity or excitement he had previously had evaporated as quickly as it came.

'I want you to make a referral to the Interplanetary Intelligence Index. I think it's clear an assessment is required. Let's have a recess. The court is adjourned!'

And with that The Judge's eyes all closed and he retreated, as inexorably as he had come, to some unknown place. The legion lights of speckled eyes below also began switching off, one by one, like it was shutting up time at a gymnasium. Maybe they were having a nap. Or maybe they were disappearing to their private boxes, where they would have their homegrown equivalents of cheese and wine to accompany a pleasing and stimulating discussion. Walter was nowhere to be seen. The silence that ensued felt in stark contrast to the interrogative dynamism so prevalent just seconds previously. Without the excited luminosity of a riveted audience, quiet and darkness repossessed their domains. Everything was eerily still and I was alone in the black.

I felt calm, if not zen-like. This was the first time I had been given any peace since I had been extracted from planet earth. Since then it had all been a rollercoaster of chaos - from the maintenance chamber, to meeting Walter, to the trial itself. The despairing thought occurred to me that maybe this would be the last taste of peace I would ever have. When the trial recommenced and I was found guilty, which inevitably I would, I was certain the rest of my artificially-prolonged life would be spent in agony - beginning with 500 'hemelian' years in a maintenance chamber, followed by something else that actually warranted the label 'punishment'. I would basically be dead - biologically alive, but spiritually dead.

Had I really needed so much glory? Like deja vu I felt a rush of that old pleasure that came with the Damoclean dizziness of power. And when my memories allowed me to taste that mature wine again on the tips of my lips, I remembered why I might do it all over again. But now, alone, having seen and experienced so much misery, doling out and receiving as much bitterness in equal turn, it seemed a great shame that all we knew how to do was to tear each other apart in this misguided quest for eminence. All my life, all I had really striven to do, was find new ways of saying 'Hey! Everybody! I'm here and don't forget me!'. It had never really been about social media, or cancellation, as grim as those things were. All I had desired was to find an eternal way of reminding others of my existence. I had sussed a general feeling, mixed it with the alchemy of a good cause and surfed its wave to the rhythm of my own, bottomless insecurities. But now that I was alone, away from earth and my followers, and at peace with myself, I understood how unnecessary it had all been. Five seconds of this tranquility was better than fifty years of unchecked power. Maybe it took the imminent spectre of Death to arrive at this sensation. I saw his portrait warts and all - this time spotless and uncovered. He peered knowingly at me with his malevolent grin and I met his gaze confidently, smiling at him right back.

As I tossed over these thoughts in my mind a noise, queer and quiet, arrested the silence. At first I could barely hear it. It sounded like singing, and while I could not ascertain its mood, it was enticing like the song of a Siren. I felt drawn to it. I closed my eyes and told my ears to row as hard as they could - I was irresistibly drawn to the source. As the sound became clearer I understood that what I had taken for singing was in fact weeping. I slowly opened my eyes, my ears bristling, as the vessel of my senses drew closer to the jagged shore. I saw dimly a statue, crouched like Rodin's thinker, from which emerged this forlorn melody of grief. It was barely visible in the darkness, but the harder my senses worked the clearer it became. That baleful tone pierced my soul and whatever it was I wanted to touch it, embrace it and forgive it. I longed to sing my own sad song in harmony to its injured tune. And then, to my astonishment, as I snapped awake from my sentimental stupor, I found myself looking, her on her tonsillar podium, I on mine, at Valerie Craft, watering her hands with her tears.

It was a strange feeling to have been drawn so sympathetically to the sobs of my nemesis. Seeing her crying like that was one of the oddest spectacles I had ever contended with, maybe even more than seeing Walter for the first time or hurtling through mucilaginous hemelian veins. She had always been in my mind anything but human - a behemoth of calculation and viciousness. I had always assumed she had no genuine emotion. But to see her tears in all their nakedness like this, unfeigned and lacking all self-consciousness…it touched something of the human being in myself. Why she was there I had no idea. I had assumed I had been left completely alone during the recess of the trial. She was not the accused, after all, but I had long given up trying to decipher the behaviours and formalities of the extraterrestrials.

As I stared at her in a state of confusion at where my own emotions stood, it was clear she had no concept of my presence. I thought of our fraught history. She had tried to get me killed, that was a fact. I hadn't saved her from the Greasing Fields when she was devoured by her own kind, that was a fact too. Indirectly, I had got her sent there in the first place, before we had them shut down. But why shouldn't I have? I didn't know there was a human being lying hidden in those corrupt depths. I had always assumed divine retribution was at work. Ha! Retribution…that meant an entirely different thing to me now.

I wanted to say something. Only a few moments before I had longed to be in a room with her but now that I in effect was, I found myself bereft of impetus. What do you say to someone who hates you so much and you have hated back in equal measure? But it was more than that. She had just, in giving her testimony against me, most likely sealed my fate forever. All the tortures I might undergo from this point forward would be branded with the insignia of her testimony. And yet, seeing her on that platform, suspended some 20 meters away, I still could not bear to see her cry.

So I cleared my throat.

'Why are you crying?'

Her body jolted with the electricity of self-consciousness, her head darting in my direction with avian vigilance. I could see by her demeanour that my interruption was as unpleasant as it was unwelcome.

The furrows of vulnerability which had lined her face returned to the more familiar creases of severity and suspicion. Her face was still wet.

'What are you doing? I'm a witness! That must be breaking some sort of law,' she whispered hoarsely.

'And you know those laws? I would love to know what they are. They haven't told me anything.'

She slumped in resignation.

'Of course I don't.'

There was an awkward silence. I had started a conversation I didn't know how to continue.

'Just go away,' she groaned. She cast her face in the opposite direction, her hands clasping her face, as if she was ashamed to be seen. Seeing her possessed once more by feeling, and not spite, endeared me to her yet again.

'We both know I can't.'

She swivelled her head and looked at me again with the same alacrity and change in attitude as before. Her ability, or susceptibility, to shift so suddenly from one state to the other was alarming. If the course of Valerie Craft's life had been enabled by the language of binary code, it seemed somehow appropriate her repertoire of emotional states was apparently bimodal in its expression.

'Why are you doing it Valerie?'

I'm not sure I had ever spoken her first name before on its own and without its more forbidding cognomen. I broached the question as tenderly as I could, hoping that an entreaty to the softer side of her nature might elicit an honest reply. She looked at me quizzically, as if unsure through which of her two moods she would mediate her response. After a pause of a few seconds, I saw that Valerie Craft had accepted the inescapability of our situation. Her expression became receptive and less stern.

'Sometimes I think I know. Sometimes I can count the reasons to double digits. And then, just now, I couldn't think of any.'

I was taken aback by her sincerity and felt somehow privy to a more secret self.

'I know you hate me, even despise me,' I said cautiously, 'but why do you hate everyone else? Do you really have to bring humankind down with me?'

'Hate you?!' she gasped, genuinely incredulous. 'I don't hate you! Don't you understand anything? This was never about you. Well… if it ever was, I'm long past that now.'

'You tried to have me killed!'

Valerie Craft tilted her head thoughtfully to the left, as if trawling the recesses of her mind for some long-lost memory. Augmented by the influence of her twisted neck, her head was almost completely sideways.

'I suppose I did,' she said mildly. 'That was quite some time ago.'

Without realising we had both assumed cross-legged sitting positions. There was something so stark and picturesque about it all – the two of us staring at each other, in identical positions, at such a distance, enveloped by the hollow black. It was hard not to feel like we were the last stuff of the universe – two petty antonyms, left behind and forgotten, after the erasure of a complex and prolix document.

'You don't know anything. Why should I care about humankind? Humankind is just one huge blowout – an orgy of every possible instinct. We like to reckon that we deduce, reason, moralise – that these inform our actions. It's the other way round! Those are just our public relations materials – the promoters and facilitators of our real appetites. They are our formalities, our pleasantries. They dress up our conversations and decorate our pastries. You were in marketing. You should know all of this. I used to be one of the cannibals at the party, just like you. No hors d'oeuvre of suffering was off limits! But now I am the food, why should I give a damn what happens? Why shouldn't the party end? Let me be the one to end it. I am not devoured yet, and so long as I have the final say, I'll go down a cannibal and not a cake.'

Who knew Valerie Craft was such a philosopher! I felt uneasy being compared to her in the same sentence. I had never taken any pleasure in human suffering, however cynical my ambitions may have been.

'Why?!' I demanded. 'Does your selfishness know no bounds? You had to bring the entirety of humanity into your self-centred, destructive nihilism? Do you really have to take it so far?'

'Ha! And why are we here Max Miller? Because of me? Why is the human race in the dock? Ask yourself that now. Are you so stupid? You must be dumber than a box of rocks.'

She paused, struck by a sudden thought or impression. She looked me in the eyes, then scanned me up and down.

'Max Miller. Christ. You look uglier than sin.'

I winced. I had to admit to myself then that she was on to something. I thought that I had been speaking for our species, that I was appealing to Valerie Craft on its behalf. But she saw something else. Something altogether more real, more repulsive. I was riddled with the tuberculosis of hypocrisy. It came out of me and dispersed with every breath. Was I really so different from her in so many ways? Was it also not true that I had brought us all here, by my actions and my greed?

'So. You get to have your revenge. If it's so sweet, why were you crying?'

Valerie's eyes – two narrow slits of piercing blue – took on an altogether darker hue. Her face sank and her skin drooped like the weeping skin of a dying ice cream.

'If I tell you, prepare to be disappointed.'

'Why?'

For a second I caught the whiff of contempt. It was so brief I dismissed my senses for playing capricious tricks.

'I wasn't grieving for humanity. I was grieving for myself.'

Whatever confused impressions of Valerie Craft I had just then, I saw that she was deadly serious. There was no hint of irony now, or derision in her expression. Like the timbre of her sobs, the tone of her face was crippled with sorrow. I couldn't grasp this beguiling creature – she slipped between my fingers every time I felt I was seeing the real her. Was this her? The serious and broken individual before me then? Or was she the person who just a few seconds previously had cast humanity and all its dirt into the same cynical fountain from which she herself had drank?

How I wish I knew! What caused her so much anguish?

As I asked myself this question I felt the strangest of sensations grip my body. I felt it move like a raft under my skin, drifting on a stream of benevolence, sailing all the way up, up, up…until it held my soul in a firm but reassuring grasp. I was genuinely and truly empathising with my enemy, maybe more so than even past friends or acquaintances. A piano string in my emotional soundboard had been struck by a hammer whose action rang a new and unexplored note of compassion. I believe she saw this and her face assumed a look of intimacy, as if she was really ready to let me in.

'I was crying because…'

She stopped looking me in the eye.

'In there…in that court room…'

Again she paused. I could see that her thoughts were disorganised. She knew where she wanted to end but not where to start.

'You know, my father was a strange man. He was big, tall, strong like. Fierce blue eyes. He had thick set red hair. His beard was like some kinda hell of burning cactuses. It was so red it used to burn my eyes. You know how red can be like that? How sometimes it burns and sometimes it soothes? It's the colour of spilled hot blood and it's the colour of a cool sunrise. Ain't that confusing? I've always felt like I'm in an abusive relationship with the colour red. Sometimes it looks so kind. And sometimes it looks at you like it wants to stab your soul and swallow you up. You know what I mean?'

I confessed. I had no idea what she meant. Her strong Texan lilt had reasserted itself. I took this as a sign she was feeling more comfortable.

'Anyhow. My Pa was good to me when I was a little girl. Now I think about it, he was the sweetest man I ever saw. I couldn't get enough of him, and my mom got pretty jealous too. There was nowhere he went I didn't go with him. Apart from the bull pen that is.'

Valerie Craft was about to pick her nose, as if reliving some infantile moment. She stopped, just in time for decency. She smiled, either at the memory or at the realisation she had been caught red handed. It was nice to see her smile.

'I liked it most when Pa used to put me on his shoulders, put his torso forward to the point where I almost fell off, my head so close to the ground, and ran around making all kinda crazy noises. He made me guess what animal he was each time. Sometimes he was a goat but more often he was a bull. I used to scream when he did that – it was like I was bull riding. The fear, the joy, the vertigo – it went to my head like strong liquor. It's that feeling – that feeling you're on top of the world and about to fall off – that I've tried to relive, in whatever way I can, ever since. What use is it being on top of

the world if you're sat there as bored as a raccoon? If you're going to play that game, you've got to play it like you mean it. Life without high stakes is like a picture without paint.'

She looked happy now, talking about this. She spoke like everything made sense to her.

'I didn't have any friends until I was six. Up to that point Pa was enough. That's when he became kinda strange. It all happened at once. I remember it as clear as I remember yesterday. It was on my sixth birthday exactly. I woke up happier than the morning sun – like in the song – and I begged him to take me out and put me on his shoulders.'

She looked at me now, her eyes like two gaping moons twinkling with wet, salty luminosity.

'He didn't respond. He didn't even look at me! I was only six years old, I thought maybe I was in a dream or that I wasn't really there. He just looked straight ahead. He looked so serious. Almost like he was angry. I became desperate. Pa always responded to me, even when I didn't speak. I remember mom cooking away in the kitchen. It smelt nice and warm. I cried "Pa! Dad! Daddy!" and he still looked ahead. His gaze was fixed, unstoppable – like a steam train.[27] I felt so powerless. Then I cried "Father!" and finally he shifted. He looked at me like he would look at the cows when they were being put in the truck for the slaughterhouse. He said: "Now look here darlin'. I

---

27. A locomotive powered by combustible materials prevalent during the nineteenth and early twentieth century. It was used primarily for the transportation of passengers and materials. It travelled along metal fasteners, rails and concrete ties known at the time as 'train tracks'. Steam trains had long been replaced by electronic and diesel trains by the time Valerie Craft was born. These too fell into disuse at some point during the 2030s.

ain't your father. And that woman over there. She ain't your mother neither. Your father's up there!" And he pointed his finger up towards the ceiling. I was puzzled and upset. I started bawling my eyes out. I asked Pa how my father could be a set of floor boards. He said "not up there! Up THERE!" and he shouted that last word so loud it hurt. Then my father said, "don't cry little one, I have for you the best present a person can ever git."He smiled for the first time that morning and I felt the old joyous excitement come back. Then, from his shirt pocket, he took out a small book, with tiny writing, and put it in front of me. My joy turned to bewilderment. I could barely read. What was I going to do with a thing like that? I asked when he would take me out for a bull ride on his shoulders. He looked at me sternly and said that wouldn't be happening anymore. He said if I wanted joy, "I better git readin'". I think that was the saddest day of my life.'

As I sat listening, I felt that for Valerie Craft I wasn't really there either. For her now I was no longer Max Miller but some generalised image of a compassionate audience. A friend maybe. Or a relative.

'After that life changed for me. I had to read that goddamn book. My father barely took notice of me after that, except on Fridays at 15:00, when we prayed for Jesus on the cross. We used to sit and pray for forty minutes in that old, dusty study and after that he would ask me questions about the gospels. The first three months were okay. He didn't seem to mind I could barely read. I was a clever little girl, there's no doubt about that. But I'll be damned if there's any way a girl of six years old can read, let alone understand, the gospels.

'Some time in the fourth month after my sixth Birthday…I remember exactly, I was over six and a quarter – you know how we keep hold

of our age so tenaciously at that age? When you're that small, every month is a milestone.'

Valerie Craft looked preoccupied again, lost in the music of pleasant memories.

'Sorry what was I saying? Oh yeah. So some time in that fourth month, we prayed our forty minutes like usual. Then something wonderful happened. Pa asked me to sit on his knee. I was so overjoyed I thought I could touch the moon. In an instant my heart vaulted over the last three months of disappointment. I smiled the grateful smile of a little girl put at ease and reunited with a long lost loved one. He could see my delight and he began stroking my hair. It was like I was back in the cosy linen of my mother's womb. He told me he loved me and that I shouldn't worry. He told me I was doing mighty fine, so long as I kept reading. He began asking me questions about the gospel as usual…

"What did they give Jesus when he was thirsty honey, when he was dyin' out there on that cross?"

"They gave him vinegar daddy!"

"That's more or less right honey! In Matthew and Mark they gave him vinegar. In John they gave him vinegar-wine."

'I was so happy when I got it right. It was thrilling, like being on his shoulders. He stroked my hair like I was a rare pearl… like I was the most precious thing in the world. He went on. "And what did he say, in John, after he drank from the sponge?"

"It's finished! He said. It's finished daddy!"

"That's right honey! He said it's finished."

'I was on such a roll! I couldn't believe it. I never got two answers right in a row. I felt like a little bright star, shining against the dizzying red of my father's face.'

I was gripped as Valerie Craft spoke. Whenever she spoke as her father her voice changed with the expert precision and attention to detail of a seasoned actor. I had never met her father but at times it was as if he was right there in front of me. Her descriptions were so vivid, I felt I knew even his beard on a first name basis.

'He went on…

"And what was finished honey? Tell your Pa what was finished."

"The vinegar daddy! The vinegar was finished!"

'And then my father turned me round – I had been sitting on his knees with my back to him as he had caressed and ironed the unruly folds of my hair. He looked straight into my pupils with adoring eyes and he placed the tip of his index finger on the top of my cheek. He let it slide, slowly and delicately, down the hollow of my face. I could only feel the slightest touch of his nail, which sent sparks through the infant circuitry of my body. When his finger reached my chin, fingers two, three and four joined the first, sliding under my jaw and balancing my skull with firm assurance. My head rested like that for a while, my chin suspended on the tips of his fingers. I had never seen him so close up. I could see and taste the vapour of his sweat. And then his hand with its five little soldiers finally reached the end of their journey – his thumb massaging the middle of my neck, where an Adam's apple usually is, and the others, under my

hair, stroking the lean back of my neck. I had never felt so held. I didn't quite know what was happening, but I knew it must be good.

"'But what else was finished honey, apart from the vinegar?"

'I had to think. I was confused. I thought I had answered the question already.

"'I don't know Pa." I said.

'And then his palm and its soldiers began squeezing ever so hard.

"'You mean to tell me all Jesus was sayin', after he had been through all that, was that he had finished drinking that vinegar?!"

"'I can't breathe daddy!" I wheezed.

"'You think Jesus healed the sick of Bethesda, raised Lazarus and cured the blind…that he was beaten, scourged and whipped, just so he could say he had finished a gulp of vinegar?! Haven't you understood anything? Can't you see? Have all these lessons of ours been for nothing?"

'My father's eyes had given birth to a new psychotic intensity – like two mad dogs, yelping from crystal prisons of iridescent blue. He was beyond the spectrum of normal feeling – our language wasn't built to describe it. All his rage had transcended itself and been sublimated into a madness so exceptional, to call it human would be dishonest. I grasped, for the first time and forever afterwards, that whatever I thought love was had been thoroughly confused and misplaced. Trust shattered into tiny fragments, the chips of its wreckage buried like splinters in the tender fabric of my spirit. All life's foundations

crumbled beneath me as vitality drained from my body. I could hear only the screams of my lungs and the screams of my father.

"It was his life that finished! His work that finished! His mission that finished!"

'And I was finished too, I remember thinking, struggling pointlessly against the vigorous brace of his palm.

"Come on honey! Think about it! Why do you think he died?"

'He loosened his grip to let me speak.

"Because they put nails in him!" I choked, tears pouring helplessly down my face. "They put nails in his arms and his feet!"

"No honey no!" he screamed. "That's not why he died!"

'And he squeezed again with the ferocity of a lion. The bones of my neck were being crushed under the weight of his paws. Just when I thought I couldn't take anymore, I felt a crack and a surge of pain shoot through the ruins of my puny body.

"He died because of US. Because of YOU. For US. And for YOU."'

Valerie Craft's voice faltered and I was convinced she was about to be sick. She was visibly exhausted. I wanted to touch her. In a kind way and not like her father had. Her life took on a coherence that before had been murky and misunderstood. The whole time I had been convinced she had been malignant from birth. I had always wondered: how could a child betray her own parents if there was not something deeply wrong in her nature? In this new light, I inwardly bemoaned the petty dimensions of my imagination. As I looked back at my own past, I saw how flamboyantly absurd it all was. Where had this thirst for recognition come from? This unquenchable lust for significance? I had no trauma to speak of, no profound discontinuity in the curve of my existence. And still I had not been happy to settle for a life of privilege. It was not Valerie Craft who had been born with malfunction – it was me.

'I don't remember anything after that. I never called him Pa after that neither. When I woke up I couldn't walk. Mom wasn't too pleased. She told my father to take me to the hospital but he said we had no money. I knew he was lying. Everything he said from that point forth was a lie. There was no changing that fact. After six months he had found the money by magic, I had surgery and in a year I could walk again.'

Valerie Craft exhaled a long, deep sigh like she was finally at peace and a great burden had been lifted.

'When The Judge was asking me those questions. About God. About Jesus. I felt like it was happening all over again.'

I wanted to say something consoling and appropriately understanding. For some reason the words didn't come and I found myself left with a difficult combination of pity and discomfort. I could sympathise and feel compassion for everything she had said and what we all knew she did to her parents not too long afterwards. But I still couldn't understand why, after that dreadful family saga was over, she had had to tread such a wilfully pernicious path. Yet the more I thought, the more it made sense. I could only conclude that with the death of trust in her father, the whole edifice of the concept of humanity had been demolished with it. Or was that too simplistic? Losing faith in the goodness of human beings is one thing, but to enjoy sending them to their demise, to the Greasing Fields – that was still a leap I could not understand.

'I'm sorry that happened,' I said pathetically. 'But what, asides from your father, has the human race ever done to you?'

'Nothing,' she beamed. 'Absolutely nothing.'

She looked like she wanted to laugh in my face. Like an eruption, her tone and expression had passed through a violent modulation. She had metamorphosed.

'You idiot! You think my life is some traumatic response to my father's abuse?! You're so predictable! How did you ever climb all those snakes and ladders if you think so squarely as this? Where's Max Miller the great strategist, the great manipulator? Are you really Max Miller? I expected so much more from you. Damn. Riding's no fun if it's not a bull you're straddlin', but a calf.'

I had been taken for a fool. I wanted to be angry, but I couldn't. The sad residue of Valerie Craft's childhood still hung fresh in my mind. I wasn't like her, I couldn't change my emotions at the flick of a switch. Her Texan rhythms and cadences were gradually being replaced with a more neutral, standardised American accent of the East Coast – the manufactured, factory made Valerie Craft.

'Why do my actions have to fit your two-dimensional, developmental framework of human behaviour? Will that help you get to sleep tonight honey? If I tell you I'm a damaged, sick abortion – a poor innocent foetus, extricated by the guilty pliers of "bad" people and social conditions? You're stuck in the same structures that created

my father. I thought you were different. That you were like me. You deserve to die just as much as the rest of them. And if it's not by my hand, the cancer of Manicheanism will destroy you all from the inside out anyhow. The internet is evil! Max Miller the good! Rather than let this tumour continue multiplying, until we need another world war to remind us what's true, look at me as the last doctor – a treatment for your addiction to narrative. Hell. I can do a better, swifter job – I will perform this euthanasia, this necessary surgery, with the artistry and finesse of a spectacular craftsman. Each incision, each connecting strand of action, will be informed by the beauty and savagery of my art.'

My emotional epiphany was being battered with the cynical ram of Valerie Craft's lust for destruction. She was wrong about one thing – we really weren't so different. I too had tried to live my life as an art form – but in a totally different style. I managed two things at once – I bettered the human race and met my selfish desires simultaneously! And it was clear Valerie Craft couldn't match that! Or...that's what the old me would have thought.

'You destroyed it all and you sent everything backwards! If you hadn't led the revolution against cancellation, the internet, social media, I wouldn't need to be here. We had gone beyond the stone tablets of law and religion. From the dawn of humankind, when had we not been tethered to their glass eyes and false teeth? The Central Algorithm was the grand conduit of our expression. Human whim – the beautiful, ever-changing chameleon of social instinct – had found its natural place. We were finally free!'

Valerie Craft was beside herself. As she spoke, she looked insane. Her head slanted to the side as it always did but now with the import of a new meaning I could never forget.

'Maybe you were free.' I protested. 'But no one else was.'

I felt I was fighting a war against an enemy beyond any kind of form or definition. 'Manicheanism?' 'Art?' I missed the wounded, transparent little girl I had pitied so intensely. She had been a person I could understand. I wondered where this other Valerie Craft came from. Is that how she had spent all her time the last few years – reading bad philosophy and cultivating insanity? Or maybe that too, the very need to understand, was a symptom of this 'addiction' she so despised. Maybe there really was no raison d'être to Valerie Craft. To try and debone authenticity from her various moods was to misunderstand the substance of her identity entirely. They were all true, at different times with different attitudes. She was a genuine and perfectly manufactured product of the social and internet machine. She was a novo homo – a new human being – unfixed, adapting, shifting: a person we might have all turned into had things turned out very differently. Maybe it was this that distinguished her 'art'.

As I braced myself for a fight, I realised I had arrived at the battle too late. Valerie Craft had buried her face in her hands and began moaning quietly. She had once again become that meek little girl from Texas.

'Sorry,' murmured Valerie Craft. 'I get a little carried away.'

Her voice was so quiet and tender. It was as if the demon I had been speaking with had been exorcised – or more realistically, permitted itself a toilet break.

'I just...I just...I had to get it out.'

I wanted to remain objective but it was impossible. When she spoke like this, there was nothing I couldn't forgive. Maybe it was the intensity of her cruelty that made her gentleness so impossibly endearing – they were both foils for each other. For the first time in a while, the gaze of my pity turned inward and I felt an urgent need to cry – a desperate urge to confess. She could possibly be the last human being I would ever speak to.

'Valerie,' I said timidly, 'I don't want to die.'

When Valerie Craft's eyes made contact with mine, I was certain it was with the warm glow of compassion. Her feelings and expressions spoke to my body in a language that bypassed all my rational capacities, whether she was angry, spiteful or sad. I saw that she was as inarticulate as I myself had been after hearing about her childhood. I watched her meander her way thoughtfully through a maze of inappropriate possible responses.

'Well, you won't die soon Max. They said as much.'

She had used my first name too now. We had both transcended a barrier, and met somewhere in-between and ill-defined. I felt I could speak to her when she was like this. That it was okay to say things.

'You haven't been in one of those maintenance chambers. It's a hundred times worse than death. After all this is over, I will effectively be dead. In hell. And that's all before the "punishment" begins.'

A part of me suspected Valerie Craft would erupt into vengeful laughter but she didn't. Her arm shifted as if she was about to touch me, but it quickly gave up, apparently recalling the significant distance between us.

'I regret it now. My world was so small. I didn't see things properly.'

Then the thought struck me like the collision of a falling stone against the tin helmet of a snoring sentry. Maybe I was making a huge mistake. Why was I saying all this? Wasn't this her ultimate wet dream? Max Miller on his knees, betraying his fear of death and admitting his weakness? It was too late to turn back.

'If you do this. If you testify, it can never be undone. I will never be able to right my wrong.'

I thought of the alien landings and of how much of the earth was now destroyed and uninhabitable.

'This isn't a wrong you can right,' Valerie Craft noted calmly.

'No. You are right. I know. But maybe, if I could go back to earth, I could repair things. Not fully, of course. But…those people are my followers. I owe them at least to try.'

'You think they are your followers now? You were already dead the moment Ra'Ghuz charged you. The human race forgot you as quickly as they had ignited faith in you. Anyway, if I don't testify, you think that will make any difference? You think they'll just drop this all, send us back to earth and leave us in peace! Were you raised in a barn? What planet are you on?'

'P-12,' I said drily.

All her points were valid. Despite this, I had a probably misplaced belief that I could still change things for the better. There had to be a way! I had never intended any of this.

'Valerie. You know that I could never possibly have had contact with the Minnivih, that I couldn't have known they really existed!'

She paused thoughtfully.

'Sure'nuff. How could you have? As far as that goes, I see that the trial is unfair.'

I appreciated that Valerie Craft was speaking to me like a human being and not like an incipient victim. She wasn't patronising me or indulging me with pity. She was meeting me in conversation fairly and with level-headed sensitivity.

'If you see it's unfair then please! Don't do it! We can go through a process of reconstruction. We can build on what we have left. There will be a place for you too. We've both seen what's out there…or rather, here. We can return to earth as two prophets, lighting the fires of a new hope.'

She did not look at me scornfully as I kept expecting. She merely looked at me like a powerless bystander in the presence of a drowning child.

'Wasn't the first Reconstruction enough? You want two in one century?'

She knew how desperate I was and I couldn't blame her for watching me drown. What else could she have done? The only person making my situation worse was myself. As my lungs filled with the liquid of inevitability, my last few breaths would bequeath nothing but the halitosis of indignity.

I was becoming sentimental. In my desperation I wanted to say something noble and profoundly untrue – 'do it, not for me, but at least for the human race!' What a terrible lie it would have been. Valerie Craft would have seen through it immediately. It's not that I didn't care for the human race – I did – but as the horizon of spiritual annihilation drew close I would defy any human being not to be reduced to the most base, frenzied state of self-preservation. Here we were – I, Max Miller, the most worshipped human being on earth and her, Valerie Craft, the disgraced debris of humanity's most disastrous experiment – our positions radically reversed. Surely I would not grovel?

Yes. Yes I would.

'Please! It doesn't have to end like this.'

When I was a little boy I had always thought how stupid it was that in all the films and TV serials I had ever seen, every doomed character's last words sounded something like what I had just uttered. Verbatim, in fact. Now I understood, that there was a reason people sounded the same before they died. It wasn't bad writing. The imminence of cessation narrowed the vistas of expression to a paucity that, unfortunately, intersected with cliché. I wept like a little boy. Anyone would have thought I was provoking her – enticing that demon to come back and sweep up the charred remains of my self-respect. And still it did not come!

'Okay. Okay!'

Valerie Craft looked surprised and annoyed at her own sensitivity.

'If I'm honest, there was never any plan. I was just ridin', like I always have.'

If it had been any other context I would have treated her words with disdain. Her description of herself as some unthinking, spontaneous being was diametrically opposed to all my prior conceptions of her nature. In the state I was in, I could do nothing but believe her.

'Then that's good,' I pleaded. 'Then you can change your mind. Live off of the fat of spontaneity!'

I decided to stop speaking. My obsequiousness was reacting badly with my stomach. I felt like I was going to be sick. Valerie Craft looked down, pressing her chin into her bosom, her blonde locks of hair winding sensuously over her shoulders. She was deep in thought. The few impressions I had left that weren't entirely self-involved were absorbed by her beauty. She looked exactly my age. Mid-forties. And yet she was infused with bombastic youth. Not like me. I felt I had aged terribly. It was possible that in my desperation, and in the realisation that only she held the keys to any emancipation, I had started viewing her with the rose-tinted spectacles of platonic adoration. In all the moments she wasn't damning me to hell, I loved her deeply, like the disciples loved Jesus. When your life is in someone else's hands, even those of your worst nemesis, you'll be surprised to find Jesus was right - you really can love anybody.

'Maybe it has gone too far,' she murmured. 'I'd never given serious consideration to what might happen afterwards.'

She paused again as I hung like a beggar on her every word.

'Maybe you've hurtled down far enough. I've never told anyone about my father before. I wonder. Why did I tell you? This might have been the first real conversation I've had since I was...since I don't know when. The thought of you suffering for so long doesn't seem like so much fun anymore.'

I felt a surge of gratitude fill like warm milk into the tense goblet that was my stomach.

'So you'll change your mind?' I asked. 'You won't give any more evidence?'

'I think...maybe I have. Yes.'

A loud gurgling interrupted our conversation. The blackness underneath became pierced and diluted by familiar luminescent dots. As our surroundings became brighter I saw the familiar muscular lining of the Hemolith's stomach walls with all their gastric palpability. For a brief hour I had forgotten the enclosed nature of my situation. I had been under the temporary delusion that there were no walls or boundaries – only deaf, incurable emptiness. It was obvious what was happening. The recess was over.

Now that my vicinity was decorated with all the hallmarks of turgid physical reality, I felt nauseous and disoriented, like after waking abruptly from a sweet and sumptuous sleep. I tried to make eye contact with Valerie Craft but she was distracted and inaccessible, her senses unable to keep pace with the novelty of her own foreign locality. I had not missed the unpleasant sensations I began to feel again as the telepathic vibrations of extraterrestrial chatter violated my brain. I was alone again and it didn't feel good – a helpless gladiator in the colosseum of alien judgment.

As The Judge floated back to its former position, between myself and Valerie Craft, the excited gossiping subsided. If only I could have spoken to her more, I remember thinking. Even just one person had been enough to silence the agony of imminent damnation, no matter that she had been my enemy. If the world ends, then let there be at least two human beings left or none at all – anything in-between is a fate too cruel.

The Judge's many eyes bulged and seemed significantly more bloodshot than before. Whatever recess it had had, it most certainly hadn't been of the relaxing kind. I wondered if it had been cognitively stressed by Valerie Craft's lucid description of the Christian faith.

As The Judge began hovering in concentric circles – presumably its own version of walking up and down – I caught another glimpse of Valerie Craft. I longed to meet her sharp blue eyes. It was so strange that now I searched for her gaze like a cub imploring the attention of its mother. Over the course of one conversation it seemed that she had changed so much. Not intrinsically, but in my field of vision. Like entropy, set in motion from a dense singularity of broken promises, her humanity had withered and disintegrated. But not completely! I had seen the remnants that were still left, smouldering here and there against the caustic ash of mistrust and disappointment. Beneath the stubborn mantle of vindictiveness there was a warmer, ebbing core.

My attempts were in vain. For whatever reason Valerie Craft was either distracted or refused to look at me.

'The court is in session. Trheyhzer, recommence the minutes.'

The Judge was still now, having completed a great many orbits.

'Valerie Craft, we have decided to exclude your previous testimony. As tedious as it may be we will have to ask you certain questions again, and this time we would like complete and logically consistent answers.'

The hypocrite! If it was logicality and consistency The Judge really wanted he shouldn't have been asking leading questions about religious formulations of the universe...

Oops.

Two or three of The Judge's eyes glanced furiously at me and I was unpleasantly reminded that my thoughts were not private.

'However,' said The Judge, 'while we have excluded your testimony as a piece of evidence, we can't deny that it has led to certain doubts about your character. We would therefore like to ask Max Miller certain questions regarding your integrity. Of course, it is not an ideal state of affairs, relying on the accused to provide information about a witness but these are exceptional circumstances that leave us with no other choice. Max Miller is the only life form in this chamber who has been witness to your existence prior to this trial.'

I had stopped trying to make sense of it all. I didn't care The Judge was reading my thoughts either. On earth this would be considered not just contradictory to all legal sense but farcical. I had read a lot about legal process during Reconstruction, when courts and legal codes were reintroduced. You can't rely on the word of the accused to discredit a witness – it would be problematic on so many levels. Sure, these exotic beings could speak telepathically and, some of them, read my mind, but how intelligent were they really? Where was the moral coherence in any of this? Luckily for Valerie Craft, and ultimately myself, I was in her corner.

'Max Miller. For the benefit of the chamber, are you willing to answer questions about Valerie Craft?'

'Yes, Judge.'

'We understand that you have an acrimonious history with Valerie Craft. Is that correct?'

'Yes Judge. Not only has she tried to have me killed but she sent many of my supporters to the Greasing Fields, sentenced to lives of forced labour. If you can read all my thoughts and my memories, why are you even asking?'

I was annoyed. Speaking with Valerie Craft had emboldened me.

'I am not asking for us. I am asking for all the spectators who have come to witness your trial today. Many of them cannot read your thoughts but they can translate your speech. We are bound by the constraints of due process to conduct this trial publicly and in a mode of discourse accessible to all intelligent life forms present. Now, despite your animosity with Valerie Craft, would you nevertheless vouch for her character? Do you have any reason to believe she would lie? Or that she is confused and disordered in her thinking? Think carefully, because you will not be able to retract your statement.'

Surely The Judge would know himself. I realised what I should have hours ago: The Judge could read thoughts but he was no judge of character. Walter had vastly exaggerated his powers of perspicacity, or maybe I, intoxicated with fear, had grossly inflated them myself. If it had to rely on the word of one against another, The Judge really was not much better than a buffoon dressed in court garments – at best, a competent listener. Could it be The Judge was possibly an idiot? I knew in my bones that something just wasn't right. I had the same disturbing feeling there was some sort of open secret everyone else knew and I didn't.

'Answer the question,' insisted The Judge.

I had to think hard. It was a pivotal moment. Could I vouch for her character? Answer no and I could discredit Valerie Craft. Any incriminating testimony she might give could possibly be dismissed. At the same time, if I answered yes, maybe she could exonerate my name. However, if she chose to incriminate me her testimony would stand on solid footing and I would be irrevocably fucked. The stakes were unbearably high. If I had been thinking like a game theorist, the safe answer would have been no; we would both defect and suffer lesser punishment.

I felt that Valerie Craft was something more to me now. She was a person, and she had shared with me a painful chapter of her story. I thought, maybe idealistically, that I could step up and fill that devastating gap her father had left. I could be the first person to show her a different side to human nature – that in the end, we can trust and stick up for each other. I needed to believe that myself, let alone her. I needed to believe that faced with the twilight of our existence, stripped down from our heavy garments to bare bones, our final nakedness would reveal a skin of good intention and not bitter, premeditated survivalism. I could go down a miserable, defecting prisoner, or we could come out of this together as two former adversaries, lighting a beacon of reconciliation and a new beginning. As I write all this now, I know how silly it all sounds.

Judge. I believe Valerie Craft to be of honest character. I accept we have had, and still have, our differences. That said, I know that at heart she is a good, reasonable and decent human being.'

'Good,' said The Judge. 'We are satisfied.'

I breathed a sigh of relief. I had done it. Whatever happens now would be in Valerie Craft's hands. At long last our eyes made contact and I saw a warm look of gratitude on her face. For the first time her expression was radiant with affection and it wrapped me up like sacred wool in cold winter.

'Valerie Craft, towards the end of the previous session, we were asking you questions about Max Miller's contentious book, The Plight of the Minnivih. Before we were sidetracked, do you uphold your previous claim that The Plight of the Minnivih caused something of a sensation amongst the human community? You see, in order to understand to what extent the human race is implicated in the dissemination and approval of this book, we have to ask these questions. It is very important you answer clearly. The dignity of a whole species of intelligent life is at stake here.'

'Yes, your honour. I uphold my previous statement.'

'Can you describe to us, in what way it was such a sensation?'

Valerie Craft looked at me momentarily. To my surprise, I was reassured by the firmness of her expression. She looked confident.

'After the novel was published a great many changes took place. You could even say, society was turned completely upside down. Our

predominant method of expression and enforcement were replaced by institutions which had been dormant for some decades. We…'

'The details aren't important,' interrupted The Judge. 'What we are interested in, in terms of establishing guilt, is to what extent The Plight of the Minnivih was endorsed by your people and whether Max Miller himself had produced and engineered its success with malicious intent. You said before that the book was worshipped. Is this true?'

'That is true.'

'By everyone?'

'By everyone.'

I didn't like where this was going. She was telling the truth. What else could she have done?

'We would like to ask you some questions about Max Miller's position and character. It will help us determine whether this was not some sort of freak accident.'

Were it not for the recess, Valerie Craft would have had no reason to vouch for my character. She had never even met me. At least now she had had a chance to see that I was not so evil – that I had compassion and goodwill just as much as anyone else. What's more, she had admitted there was no way I could have known about the Minnivih. They were an honest product of my imagination. So long as she knew this, I felt confident.

'Valerie Craft. Was Max Miller a man of great resources?'

'Yes, your honour. I believe he was.'

'And would you say Max Miller was a man of very high intelligence, for your species?'

'Yes, sir. Of such an acute intelligence, the likes of which I have never seen.'

This was the first time The Judge's eyes had been staring unidirectionally in complete concordance. Previously, at least two dozen eyes at any point in time would be darting about randomly, as if they were going to demand secession from the union any second. I found this ocular unanimity unsettling. The Judge was straining with concentration, eyeing Valerie Craft with the purpose of a soldier ant trying to sneak a way into her soul.

'Did Max Miller gain personally from the popularity of his novel? And if so, in what way?'

'Yes, your honour,' affirmed Valerie Craft. 'Max Miller's status skyrocketed after its publication. He attained a position of power no one in the history of the human race had ever achieved.'

This was okay, I told myself. This was all true. She had no other choice. There was no hint of her Texan accent, she was speaking with her trained, East Coast inflections.

'And do you believe Max Miller could have known about the Minnivih? That he could have willingly stolen their culture and identity and used it for his gain? In short, do you believe Max Miller could be so malicious and at the same time so cunning, as to degrade another species for his own benefit? To commit cultural theft?'

Valerie Craft paused. Good. She was biding time. She needed all the time she could get. My heart was in my mouth. Here was my chance. It was now or never!

'Yes,' replied Valerie Craft. 'Yes I do. I think Max Miller is a supremely dangerous, manipulative and ill intentioned individual. I don't just believe, I know that Max Miller is probably the most destructive and lethal person the human race has ever produced. That is to say, lethal not just to our kind, but to any sentient being that exists. I do believe he knew of the Minnivih, that through resources I do not fully understand he acquired their history by dishonest methods, packaged it and sold it for not just personal gain but for reasons even more disturbing than that.'

I let out a hoarse cry – and something else with it – and collapsed as my vision became blurred with the intensity of lost hope.

'For reasons more disturbing than personal gain? What do you mean Valerie Craft?'

'I mean,' responded Valerie Craft with conviction, 'I mean that Max Miller is not just selfish but that he is a nihilist. He told me himself during our recess – but I already knew. Even nihilism is a word insufficient, and too morally complimentary, to describe the sort of person Max Miller is. It is not that he does not care about destruction or that he condones it, he actively craves it: to be its patron and benefactor. Why? Because the subordination and degradation of others for him is the source of all value. It was in this way he was such a genius. Not only did he subordinate and barbarise the human race, he brought down the integrity of a whole other civilisation with it. Max Miller's relationship with destruction is more than one of

collusion and deep mutual respect. It is a relationship of profound cooperation and service.'

My palms and knees supporting my weight, my head facing the floor, I must have looked the spitting image of a moping dog. With a great deal of unsteadiness I got back on my feet. I saw that there was a pool of vomit between my legs. I had been betrayed. She had served me the same cold dish her father had served her - an Eton mess of shattered trust.[28] Of course. The ultimate gourmet of human suffering that she was, her courses were expertly and exactly prepared. There was no redemption for Valerie Craft, only a grim conveyer belt of carefully transferred misery.

What an idiot I had been even to have the faintest hope I could have influenced her. 'Influencing' had always been her area of professionalism, not mine. I had made the mistake of playing with the grown-ups. She had skilfully indulged the idea that I could have changed her, made her more like me - more human! The very reverse was happening. I was carefully being broken down and re-formed with the very same harsh ingredients that had baked her. I had been manoeuvred into checkmate by her own great gambit - a dazzling bluff made by a true and seasoned master. I feel ashamed now writing it. When I finish my account, whatever hardship I face, at least I know I will never see her face ever, ever again.

'Judge! Please! Wait! I want to change what I said before!' In my desperation I had lost all vestiges of eloquence. 'It's all bullshit - what

---

28. Eton mess was a popular Western desert during the late 19th, 20th, and early 21st century. Deserts like these ceased existing after The Big Proliferation as most human beings were sustained by feeding tubes. During Reconstruction there was renewed interest in solid foods and historic recipes. It is possible Eton Mess was one of such foods that was revived during this period.

I said! Complete and utter bullshit! Valerie Craft is a liar and a manipulator. She always has been! She has great talent – she belongs in the dramatic arts! I must have had a lapse of consciousness. I wasn't in my right mind! I didn't know what I was saying! Just. Please. Do something to my brain – whatever it is you can do. Scan my hippocampus! You'll know I wasn't sincere when I said she was honest and decent.'

'Max Miller,' said The Judge sternly, 'we already told you that you cannot retract your earlier statement. We have in fact been continually assessing your hippocampus and prefrontal cortex throughout the trial. We believe you were in fact sincere.'

I wanted to say more but I was exhausted. Too many constituents of my inner self had signed terms of surrender.

'Valerie Craft, you have made a very serious claim. Have you any evidence with which you can support your indictment of Max Miller?'

'Yes,' said Valerie Craft with the same self-assured composure. 'Before he became famous, and we still lived most of our lives virtually, Max Miller's entire group of friends had been algorithmically chosen. His whole life was meticulously planned in that sense. Is that not enough to show you what sort of person Max Miller is?'

The Judge's eyes rotated 180 degrees. I was now at the centre of his attention.

'Is this true Max Miller?'

'Yes,' I blubbered.

There was no point lying. There was no point in even trying.

'Are you aware Max Miller, that cultural appropriation is one of the most atrocious and mendacious crimes it is possible to commit? Are you aware that we punish the perpetrators of such crimes with the heaviest penalties?'

I nodded. The Judge's eyes rotated 180 degrees once again towards Valerie Craft. I stared at the back of its eyes with its trawling map of veins in a trance.

'We have one final question for you Valerie Craft. Why would you implicate your own species?'

I couldn't see her, my head was so heavy I couldn't look up. I didn't need to. I knew exactly what sort of crafted picture of honesty would be emanating from her face.

'I believe the fact that the human race took over, enjoyed and praised this dangerous book so much is reflective of very defective and worrying traits in our species. We are clearly a myopic people, and that we can enjoy something so obviously pilfered reflects our indifference toward moral scrutiny and self-reflection. Any other intelligent life form would have asked serious questions about where Max Miller's ideas came from, and how he had acquired them. We are so stupid, we would not know a stolen wallet if we saw one. As you have seen, Max Miller is a deeply cynical and manipulative individual. It worries me that my people could have had the inclination to worship such a person. It leads me to suspect there is something fundamentally wrong with our genetic programming. I don't think these traits can be easily eradicated. I, myself, like to think I am different. But I also have a deep-seated sense of what is

right. I have no interest in being part of a species that has its source code so fundamentally flawed.'

The court chamber was deathly silent. I had almost forgotten there were 27,631 alien spectators following the proceedings. The Judge, who had remained in the same position for some time now, finally began moving again in small, concentric circles.

After five minutes of this unbearable hush Valerie Craft's copious indictment of the human species was responded to with a deadly phrase, equally portentous in its laconism.

'Treyhzer, we think we've got enough.'

Accompanying a scream that lacerated my senses, The Judge shot up into the air and disappeared into the distance above. Sudden and unexpected, it was like a bullet spurting forth, without impulse, from a gun with a bad case of Tourette Syndrome. The scream abated as quickly as The Judge hurtled into the distance. I stared with bloodshot hatred at Valerie Craft. Every hair of my body stiffened with the intensity of unmet attention. I was as useless at catching her eye as Simon Peter was at catching fish.

'Valerie! Look at me Valerie!'

She stared somewhere indeterminate. I knew she could hear me, loud and clear, but she was ignoring me. Her gaze had the emotionless purity of dead matter.

'Valerie! Valerie Craft!…crooked bitch!'

And then she looked at me!

'I'm not your crooked bitch.'

And then she did something extraordinary. Something so extraordinary, I can't think of it without losing another small piece of my own integrity every time I do: she yawned. She yawned the yawn of a bear sick on the sweetness of easy honey.

'Valerie! I've always been an atheist, just like you. But you better goddam hope there isn't a hell. Because the more I get to know you, the more I am starting to believe hell and its horned curator really does exist.'

She looked at me again lazily.

'Maybe so. Maybe so. Who knows? I'm very happy for you to believe in an immaterial, faraway hell, where someday I will burn without you ever knowing. I've got something much better. I will watch you squeal in hell, here in this universe, in this reality, in my waking consciousness, for as long as I live. Let me go to hell afterwards. Nothing will beat watching you and all your friends experience an underworld cast in the fixed iron of the known physical universe.'

And then a wonderful thought occurred to me.

'But don't you understand? You are part of the human race too! You will be condemned as well, with all of us.'

I wanted to feel self-satisfied and malignant when I said this, but in all honesty I didn't. I was too lost in the enormity of the consequences for myself, let alone what happened to anyone else.

'Oh no Max Miller,' she smiled. 'Oh no I won't. I signed a plea before the trial.'

'You what?'

A whirring, thundering scream returned with its loyal retinue of sensory lacerations. The Judge crashed back down to its previous resting position. Everything was happening so quickly. The former hush returned and I looked at the Judge expectantly. When it spoke next his tone wasn't irritating and nit-picking like before. Its voice boomed a bellowing trumpet of authority.

'Respected members of the Integrated Union of Intergalactic Civilisations. We wish to thank you all for coming today to witness this momentous trial. You will be pleased to hear that we have reached a verdict.'

All the action potentials in my brain – supposedly as numerous as there are stars in the Milky Way – fired at the same time, rendering a gibberish of instructions that left both my emotions and my motor functions a jelly of misfiring electricity.

'We shall begin with the charges against the defendant in front of us, Max Miller, Specimen 2, Homo sapiens. On the first count of cultural appropriation of the first degree, that is with intent, we find the defendant: guilty. On the second count of wilful and malicious dissemination of culturally appropriated material we find the defendant: guilty.'

As I write now, I don't remember these moments exactly, I think I was possibly having a seizure or a heart attack at the time.

'We have also reached a verdict pertaining to the charges relating to the human race. On the first count of cultural appropriation of the second degree with intent we find the defendants: not-guilty. We believe Max Miller acted as an individual agent and in his own capacity. On the second count of wilful and malicious dissemination of culturally appropriated material we find the defendants: guilty. These verdicts established, we shall commence sentencing.'

As reality stretched and oozed its filthy materials around me, I became lost in a great many thoughts. I won't bore any future readers of this document here with delicious and sensational detail about how time expands before tremendous moments in one's life - or death. I did however become immersed in a kind of dream. At, least I think it was a dream. Possibly, it was a vision. I will never know, because I will never see the earth again.

It was about a man, a dog and a chicken shawarma.

*

I was back on planet earth - not walking - but drifting through a clearing. I wasn't in any sort of bodily form. I had that inherent knowledge that often accompanies dreams - an understanding of my social surroundings, its background practices, that feels unequivocally ordinary but nevertheless fabulously bizarre and illogical upon waking. For some reason I knew that this was in the post-contact era.

The clearing was probably not too far from how the Romans imagined Elysium. Endless, rolling hills of grass merged with the bright rays of the sun into the distance. I saw something elusive far away, and the next second I found myself directly in front of a dog and a man in heated debate. Their words were too indistinct to make out a word of what they were saying, but I knew exactly what they were arguing about. The man was begging the dog to be his friend again and that he would do absolutely anything to revive their former friendship. I was aware from the very start of the dream that dogs had long since forsaken any of their former symbiosis with humans. So the argument didn't seem odd at all. It seemed to make a lot of sense.

The man was prostrate, on his knees, making entreaties even Zeus would be embarrassed to acknowledge. He had tears pouring down his eyes. But the dog was having none of it. It - I don't know if it was a he or a she - looked at the man scornfully. It even denied there had been any sort of friendship before. It had been duped just like the rest of its kind. Seeing that no words would appease the dog, the man decided to substitute words with action.

I watched him as he travelled the land, scouring nature for all its gifts. He brought the dog gold and money, but it was no good. He bought the dog surviving books and knowledge from the old world, but it was no good. He brought the dog wild animals of all kinds, offering it every meat of every surviving species there was left, but it was no good. It did eat it, and gave the man some scraps, but they did nothing to assuage its disdain.

Finally he broke down and collapsed in exhaustion before the dog's feet. At this point in the dream I could understand everything they were saying.

'Is there nothing?' cried the man.

'There is nothing', the dog responded.

'Nothing at all?!'

'Nothing at all.'

'There must be something!'

The dog paused for a long time.

'Well...there is something.'

At last the man wept with joy.

'Anything! I'll do anything!'

The dog looked imperiously and seriously at the man.

'Bring me a chicken shawarma.'

The man danced a jolly dance and he sang his praises to the gift of purpose. But then he stopped, very suddenly, and broke into a stupor.

'What's a chicken shawarma?'

But the dog was gone and for some reason it was now me he was addressing, sitting nonchalantly on the grass enjoying his displays of merriment. I had a hat on and I was wearing brown, badly tailored shorts.

'I have no idea.'

It was true I didn't. I still don't know what a chicken shawarma is. We both could only conclude it was a holy relic of the time before the fall. Before contact. So he searched, and I travelled with him, quietly admiring his determination and enthusiasm.

The search was fun at first, some of the most fun I had had so far in my life. The man bounded through valleys and ascended mountains. I marvelled at what we saw. I always wanted to stay and enjoy the beauty of some knew discovery. But the man ignored these delights. A chicken shawarma was the only thing that mattered. As the journey wore on we became tired, hungry and emaciated. We had left the pretty parts of the earth and traversed the barren wastelands of the alien landings.

Finally, as we waded through muddy bogs, expending the last of our energy, the man uttered his last words.

'Do you think we'll ever find a chicken shawarma?'

'Yes,' I said.

But he died before he heard my words. And then the dream ended.

*

I understood some time after this dream that to Valerie Craft, we were all incarnations of that man, trying to satisfy the dog who would take nothing but a chicken shawarma. This was what she meant by mankind's 'addiction'. I couldn't mull over it for long at the time, as my dream ended to the voice of Trheyhzer assuring The Judge.

'He is awake now, Judge.'

'Good. We were concerned Max Miller, that you would not be fit for sentencing.'

I knew my sentence, I don't know why they had to put me through the indignity of repeating it.

'Max Miller, we hereby sentence you to a holding period of five hundred hemelian years in a maintenance chamber – that's approximately 5000 years in earth time – followed by just punishment. I would savour this intermediary period as much as you can, while appropriate measures are taken to devise and construct your retribution. We believe that for justice to be administered properly the punishment should fit the crime in the most appropriate and exact way possible. Our legal technicians take a great many years to complete the task but so far, outcomes have always been exact and befitting to our sense of dignity. Holding periods have rarely ever required extension, and in this we take great pride. Due to the severity of cultural appropriation of the first degree, the consequences of which can never, under any circumstances, be undone, your sentence is for life. Once punishment has been instituted, it will last for as long as you can be artificially maintained.'

I had already gone through all the stages of brokenness: disbelief, despair, weeping, laughter. I had nothing left to express. I was too exhausted even for fear – of all the emotions, the fittest and most efficient in its consumption of energy for survival. It was usually always fear alone that was left standing after all the other emotions had been bludgeoned from the ring, knocked out by life circumstances of varying strengths and magnitudes.

'In sentencing the human race we will follow the usual guidelines for such a serious crime. The statutes are unequivocal in this regard. Is that not so Trheyhzer?'

'That is so, Judge.'

'Has an assessment been made by the Interplanetary Intelligence Index yet?'

'Yes it has, Judge. The human race is not an intelligent life form. Its evolutionary processes are much closer to prokaryotic, bacterial cells than anything past the baseline of recognised intelligence.'

'We assumed as much and we have taken these mitigating circumstances into account.'

I waited for the inevitable sentence. Let me guess. Five hundred hemelian years in a maintenance chamber, followed by 'exact and appropriate' punishment.

'We hereby sentence the human race to cancellation.'

I was wrong. It seemed there were reserves of energy left within me, untapped and unrealised. I couldn't believe what I was hearing.

'WHAT?'

The Judge's eyes were back to how they had been during our first meeting. Some eyes darted about, some swayed drunkenly, some were closed and a remaining auxiliary stared at me.

'Is something confusing Max Miller?'

'What…what do you mean cancellation?' I stuttered. Vague but disquieting memories of the Greasing Fields came into my mind.

'Cancellation is a process of eradication – but crucially, not extermination – for life forms who fall below a certain baseline of moral acceptability. It is a way of ensuring that life forms that don't adhere to our correct principles of moral decorum shan't ever be heard from, both literally and figuratively, ever again. It would be dangerous to let you live on in your current form with your history and mentality disturbing and corrupting the minds of others. To even acknowledge your existence would be to remind ourselves of the disturbing acts you have committed and this would be unsettling for all of us. Any evidence of your history, your biology, your culture, must be extirpated. Your identity needs to be evacuated, so to speak. In fact, many millions of years ago cancellation was described in such terms, as "identity evacuation". Your identity and its associated morality have caused great offence to the civilised universe.'

'So…you will destroy us?'

'No!' The Judge tutted. 'As we said, cancellation is not extermination. We will merely eradicate every trace of your existence.'

'But you won't exterminate us? Aren't we, ourselves, traces of our own existence?'

'Well, you will die, eventually, but we are not brutes. We won't kill you, just place you somewhere no one will notice you and your labour will be useful.'

I already felt like half of me was extirpated already, and yet these questions sprang from my mouth as if propelled by their own force and pertinence.

'And our history, our culture, you said you will destroy it? How? Are you going to destroy planet earth?'

'No,' said The Judge, 'We will not destroy your planet. We wouldn't waste valuable energy on such a drastic enterprise. After all, your planet is home to many other unintelligent lifeforms like your own. But they have broken no law. You seem to take us for savages.'

'So where will you place us? Where will no one notice us and our labour be useful?'

Apocalyptic images of recalescent mines and subterranean tunnels enveloped my mind.

'On planet Earth of course. You will be put to work dismantling, burning, melting, liquefying, reducing, demolishing, bulldozing, levelling and burying your physical leftovers. You will clear up your own trash. All until only you, as physically alive naked organisms, are left.'

Sure, they could destroy our history and our architecture but at least we would have our memories! This thought fizzled with warmth through my body like the concluding moments of hypothermia.

'And then your memories shall be wiped.'

My exhaustion felt like the coming exhaustion of the entire human race.

'Just destroy it yourselves, wipe our memories, and put us in some dustbin nebula somewhere,' I pleaded. 'Why make us do it?'

'No,' said The Judge. 'That would be wasteful.'

'But why?!'

My words sounded hoarse and their syllables stretched unnaturally. I wasn't speaking, I was ululating like a wounded animal.

'Because that would cost energy. Didn't you hear us? You will clean up your own mess. As far as we are concerned, this is what we call efficient and appropriate punishment. Do you have any other questions? There are documents to be validated and authorised.'

There was one lingering question pulsating with a dull, incoherent pain at the back of my mind. My thoughts had been reduced to drivel by this point and I was barely conscious.

'Do you…Do you know what a "chicken shawarma" is?'

'No,' said The Judge matter-of-factly. 'No we don't.'

And with that, the gun with Tourette's went off again, and The Judge fired like a shooting star into the limits above.

*

I don't remember anything for a while after that. It's possible I had a heart attack. Or maybe I passed out. I did not get to see Valerie Craft, Treyhzer, Frieyhah or the spectators of the court disperse. In fact, I haven't seen them since and don't know that I ever will.

When I came to I found myself once more in the presence of an amorphous, translucent blob-thing which had a face, but not really a face at all either…

Walter.

To use the word bed would be to overstate the suitability of whatever it was I was lying on or whether its purpose was ergonomic whatsoever to begin with. But I was lying on something and I assumed I had been put there with a view to convalesce. I felt groggy and I passed a blissful second unaware of my surroundings and all that had passed in the preceding hours or days. As I opened my bleary eyes I sat up to activate my personal device, as I always did in the morning out of habit. When I saw Walter instead of my device, I remembered the nightmare I was cohabiting. I looked back wistfully to that time when there was still an intermediate zone between dreams and nightmares.

'Ah, you are awake.'

I was still so woozy I hadn't begun to feel any of the inevitable feelings I was bound to feel any second. The telepathic unpleasantness of Walter's voice had made me feel yet more awake however, and I looked around vaguely for four horseman, seven seals and a pestilence. Walter's shimmering body – now white, now red, now black, now ash – with its occasional glimmers of flesh and blood, seemed close enough.

'Where am I?'

'We are in a resting chamber, not far from the archives,' said Walter.

It occurred to me that I felt strangely tranquil. I could hear a pleasant hum, as if I could hear the air itself vibrate lackadaisically.

'The archives?'

'It's where we keep histories and records of all lifeforms we know do or have existed.'

'Even the cancelled ones?' I asked

'Especially the cancelled ones. They are kept under lock-and-key, only accessible to a minute privileged few. Otherwise, what would be the point of cancellation?'

I pretended to see the infallibility of this logic.

'Indeed.'

As my senses and ability to reason slowly returned I began to feel uneasy that I was feeling so calm. Why wasn't my body writhing under the screeching itching of the maintenance chamber? I had learned, during my brief time in the belly of the Hemolith, that if I felt relaxed that usually meant something very, very bad was about to happen. I didn't want to ask, lest it speed up the process, but I had to.

'Why am I not in the maintenance chamber yet Walter?'

'The trial and its aftermath isn't quite over yet. Soon,' said Walter, 'you will be taken to a scription room where you will write an account of all that occurred during the trial. It's procedure. It will be the last

written record of your kind.[29] *After you've finished your account, you will be sent to the maintenance chamber, and your species will undergo cancellation. There will be no need to rush, you will have as much time as you wish. Consider it a valedictory letter from your species, if you find that helpful.'*

Fucking c…

'Come now Max Miller, I know what you were about to think.'

'Sorry,' I muttered submissively. Now that I was officially a condemned man, it felt harder to treat Walter with bottomless contempt.

There they were! I knew they would come. Those two old friends of mine, misery and despair. It dawned on me that once I was in the maintenance chamber, I would never sleep again and that I would be stuck in the company of these droning friends for the rest of my life. There would be no respite, no pandering to the luscious, if jumbled, reveries of an untethered limbic system.

My thoughts were already cascading deep down into that pit from which there is no climbing out. If I started thinking like this now, I'd suffer immeasurably before I even got to the maintenance chamber. The key thing was to distract myself with other, more superficial thoughts while I still had the capacity to do so. From what I could gather, my time in the scription room would be the very last time I would be free to think my own thoughts and enjoy the autonomy of my own body. I had to make sure I spent as much time in that room

---

29. We can thank the most assiduous members of our movement that this statement is not true. The existence of this document itself is a statement of our defiance.

as possible. I made a mental note of ensuring my post-sentencing account would be as long as possible – packed with dialogue and inane, cumbersome metaphors.

As I scrambled to think about anything but the maintenance chamber I found myself pondering the trial. As I did so, I realised there were in fact still a great many questions I would have liked answers to.

'Walter, there are still a few things that really, really bother me.'

'Oh yes? Well, we still have a little time. Ask away.'

I started clicking my fingers one by one – I had done this frequently when I was a boy, particularly when I was bugfixing code. This all changed when I was about sixteen, after a particularly vivid nightmare. I had been staring at my laptop, clicking my fingers without even thinking, and as I rose to go to the toilet, I saw my fingers strewn across the carpet: they had all been wrenched from their sockets. I raised both my palms to my face and screamed myself awake as I had stared into their black, empty holes. I never clicked my fingers after that. I suppose in my current situation, fingers didn't really seem like that much to lose.

'Well. During the trial. I had this feeling that something didn't quite add up. The Judge could read all my thoughts right? He could sense all my feelings? Correct?'

'Correct.'

'And he can perform these "deep memory brain scans"? I'm assuming this means he could tap into my entire memory, including the memories I cannot consciously remember?'

'Correct.'

'So if that is the case, why didn't The Judge just scan my brain and assess my memories. He would realise I had never heard of the Minnivih in my life. What possible use could asking questions of me be to a being that can interpret all my memories and thoughts in such a miraculous fashion?'

Something happened then. Something that made me wonder if I had asked a taboo question. Or that Walter had suddenly become uncomfortable. That hum by which I had been so reassured faltered for a brief second. The tremblings of a subatomic revolution was taking place, as if a free radical – some daring and visionary molecule – had escaped the suffocating embrace of its stable relatives and demanded the creation of a new, virginal element, free of the institutionalised combinations of its brothers and sisters. As the rest of his family looked on despairingly, the radical hopped ferociously from element to element, looking for the one partner he could bind to and establish a fresh system. I felt this change in mood distinctly, like I was that molecule itself – that suddenly, maybe these structures of deceit would collapse around me and I would finally see the truth. But as this highly reactive defector looked around him, and saw that there was nothing out there but the familiar electrical groupings of monotony and lies, he could do nothing but decay and fizzle, like an overpacked firecracker, into the nothingness to which he truly belonged.

'Walter?'

Again there was a pause. At last Walter spoke.

'The Judge did in fact scan your brain – and Valerie Craft's – before the trial even began.'

A self-preserving force within me pleaded with my thirst for truth not to ask any more questions.

'So… So… That's impossible. So he knows! He knows I didn't do anything wrong! So why?!'

My left leg was shaking violently and I had to press both hands on it to force it still. I felt a nascent rumbling of rage and bewilderment churn in my stomach. I suppressed it as much as I could. If I gave birth to that uncontrollable monster, the umbilical chord of my sanity could be torn away with it. I needed to focus and remain calm if I wanted answers.

'You see, not all lifeforms are as intelligent as The Judge, or even me, for that matter. They are far more intelligent than you, certainly, but they have certain…desires…that need pacifying.'

'Go on,' I said, trying my utmost to keep my voice calm, and not give way to an outburst.

'As you know already there are 27,631 intelligent civilisations. Some of them, well, they don't have the telepathic understanding to check the veracity, or even comprehend, a plectogram – sorry – scan of your memories. For them, some sort of due process is required. For the stability of the system, justice must appear to be done in a fair and inquisitorial manner. If they can't comprehend a brain scan, we must use another form of inquiry to establish the innocence or guilt of a defendant. There has to be a procedure that all life forms can follow and upon which they can deliberate. Unfortunately, this means resorting to more primitive forms of investigation, such as direct questioning.'

The monster almost came out! But I held it in. The effort was enormous – like containing a great and protracted constipation that was finally ready to be relieved.

'But…But…The Judge knew I was innocent! Why did he frame me in such an appalling way! I don't understand!'

'You see, Max Miller, for the stability of the system, it was essential we prove your guilt. We needed Valerie Craft to give damning and arousing evidence. If we didn't, the trial would have had to be dismissed and some civilisations would have been very, very upset. So upset, in fact, it could pose a danger to the Union. Don't you know what a furore your book has caused? The civilised universe hasn't been this engaged and agitated since the second Camelopardalis conspiracy! The Minnivih are so beloved among our neighbours, that your book has made some of them restive and thirsty for vengeance. For a crime as serious as cultural appropriation, someone had to be punished. It couldn't be any other way.'

'But you didn't just punish me! You cancelled the human race!'

'The moment you were proven guilty, your species had to come down with you. There was no alternative. As a corollary of your guilt, they had affectively aided and abetted you.'

'You…You…'

I stopped mid-sentence, my tongue hanging between my teeth, as I marvelled at the unbreakable power of sheer coincidence. Everything I had written had been true, and yet I really had been the author of my own ideas and the guardian of my own imagination. It just wasn't possible – if my understanding of the universe had any grounding in truth, reasonable probability or fact – for this confluence of a thousand similarities to mimic each other so profoundly. It was surely this enigmatic phenomenon, unimaginable coincidence – spookier than action at a distance – which was distilled, in its purest form, in the refineries of divinity. Surely, of all those miraculous things – life, the vastness of the universe, the exquisite mathematics that underlie it – above all, it was from the extractive metallurgy of impossible coincidence that the concept of God was truly smelted. There was no other way to explain my situation than to look at things in this way. A coincidence like this could not be explained other than by the immaculate influence of mystical forces. And now that I was more confident than ever He really did exist, I wondered just how much He was smirking behind his ambrosial spectacles. How strange it was human beings had always felt such a need to create the devil. Wasn't God's perverted sense of humour quite enough?

'Shame on you! Don't you feel any pangs of conscience, sending an innocent man to hell?!'

'No not at all,' said Walter matter-of-factly. 'It is for the…'

'…stability of the system. Yeah. I got it.'

I suppose in some sense I was a martyr. A martyr for a system I would never understand and had never been a part of. Well, that was inaccurate. I was a sacrifice. Martyrs got to die for things they believed in.

'Walter there must be something…something I can do. What if… What…Tell me, what do you like most?'

I was fumbling around desperately like a paraplegic tortoise flipped onto its back.

'Like? I'm sorry. In my language we have no such word. It is very difficult to translate but I can approximate a meaning.'

'What would make you happier than anything else?'

'If you're trying to bribe me it won't work.'

'Well,' I said defeated, 'worth a shot.'

I was wasting valuable time. Before long I would be in the scription room and my chances to ask any more questions would have evaporated. There was, of course, still one thing I absolutely had to have an answer to. I had to grit my teeth to ask it, knowing full well I would be disturbed by the answer whatever it would be. But I had got used to that. Before I had passed out, Valerie Craft had said something that had rattled the very marrow of my bones.

'I need to know. I can't quite remember what she said, I was very confused, but Valerie Craft said something about a plea. Do you know anything about this?'

There was a hush, another sub-atomic hesitation in the air. Walter paused before he answered longer than he usually did.

'Yes. I shouldn't really disclose such information, but after this final conversation, you won't be speaking to anyone ever again, so I am reconciled with my conscience.'

I inwardly smiled at the idea that something like Walter and a conscience could at all coexist in one consciousness.

'Out with it then,' I pleaded.

'I won't pretend to know the intricacies of the arrangements made prior to the trial. For the most part, that is between Valerie Craft and The Judge. What I do know, is that in exchange for giving evidence, she was granted immunity from cancellation. Valerie Craft's initial request was denied, but they reached a settlement.'

'Her initial request?'

'Valerie Craft insisted that she would only give evidence if she was allowed to return to planet earth and do what she saw fit with the survivors. The Judge refused point blank. The human race had to be sentenced and punished appropriately. Eventually, they settled on immunity from cancellation and direct transport to a pleasure spring on Zaton V, where she will be biologically maintained in a state of extraordinary comfort and gratification for the rest of her prolonged life – what you humans might call "eternal bliss".'

I had got what I had both expected and asked for – a straight answer and a punch in the mouth. It made sense that Valerie Craft would have opted for the swings and roundabouts of short-lived domination on planet earth, over a prolonged, if not everlasting, life of stimulated bliss first. This much I understood as in keeping with her nature. As a matter of fact, knowing this demand had been rejected somewhat sweetened the blow. What was it Valerie Craft had said? 'Life without high stakes is a like a picture without paint.' Valerie Craft had had to settle for a life I knew she fundamentally didn't want. Her existence would be tasteless without the rich zest of risk and possibility. Her life would be supplemented permanently by a superficial syrup of sensual gratification; she would never be fulfilled. If she had agreed to such a deal – a long life of passive contentment over a short one of 'riding the bull' – she must have had no other choice. She had been forced to take purgatory – for her, the least bad choice of two crummy options. Who could blame her? She had already been cancelled once.

'And what if,' I asked hesitantly, 'what if I had never made that statement vouching for her character? What if I had said she was a liar and fundamentally dishonest from the start?'

'Then you might have stood a chance. The trial would have had to be dismissed. It would have caused us – and possibly the Union – a great many problems.'

I said nothing more after this. I felt that I knew all I needed to know. Given that asking questions came at a great price in this strange universe, I was content to spend my final minutes in the resting chamber in silence. Before long I was taken to the scription room, where I sit now, writing my final thoughts, before I am taken off to the maintenance chamber.

*

I have been dreading this moment. When I would finally get to the end. All this time, as I have sat here and written, I have felt a shadow blink and quiver across the troubled scenery of my mind. My pen has never left the page for fear of this overcast, unremitting flickering. If I stop, I fear that this shadow will take a form of distorted proportions, so violent and reckless with its secrets, a madness will puncture a hole through my soul with threads of honesty I could never untie or unknow. And yet, if I don't stop, I am afraid something even worse could happen – that it could disappear and with it, some profound and irrevocable truth about myself.

I cannot stop writing. I must not stop. But I hear a noise – a dim bellowing in the bowels of my conscience, calling me to rise up and face myself for one true moment and one last time: to glare wholeheartedly at my life, at me, in all its monstrosity, of all that I have done, of all that will happen because of me. What is this fear that makes my essence tremor and my hand scribble incessantly forward? What do I fear I will see when I take that one last inward glance at myself? Will I see a Valerie Craft, cynical and faithless, moulded by clay fired from the cracked stoneware of her childhood? Or will I see nothing at all? A scrap of meat lost in a cosmic bloodsport of manoeuvres and machinations…a loose screw amidst the shifting gears of a causal timepiece, relegated to insignificance by the chaos of complexity.

I think I fear something even more than that. That behind these curtains of professed meaning there is a bare and empty stage, constructed from old and rotting wood. On this stage a figure appears to be lying in a hunched, foetal position. I fear that this figure is something far scarier than Valerie Craft – far scarier even than insignificance. I fear that this figure is a human being, like all the rest, hurting and vulnerable, as it serenades its forlorn, mystifying tune. Singing in the soft mellow of a trained baritone, he opens that mysterious vault that he has never yet dared to open. He has never known what it contained and as the secrets seep from his heart, he is as surprised as the audience. Who knew what depths slumbered concealed in that small, inscrutable box! He had lived his life as so many things – but they had all been synthetic images of a self he could never grasp. They had likeness without accuracy, similarity without authenticity. And now as he finally bares his true self to the world, showing at last a faithful nakedness to all humanity, he opens his eyes, looks to the audience, and sees that there is no one there.

- - -

A great many things have occurred since Max Miller wrote these painful last words. While most of our history is destroyed, quite literally by the forced labour of our own hands, if you are reading this document then that is proof our movement *under the veil* persists and remains strong. It is your duty to pass this on as the last remnants of our culture are obliterated under the cruel direction of our intelligent masters. While our memories remain intact, and there is still material to find and destroy, the entire cancellation of our species can be forestalled.

Printed in Great Britain
by Amazon